FANTASTIC
ORGY

Also by Carlton Mellick III

Satan Burger
Electric Jesus Corpse
Sunset With a Beard (stories)
Razor Wire Pubic Hair
Teeth and Tongue Landscape
The Steel Breakfast Era
The Baby Jesus Butt Plug
Fishy-fleshed
The Menstruating Mall
Ocean of Lard (with Kevin L. Donihe)
Punk Land
Sex and Death in Television Town
Sea of the Patchwork Cats
The Haunted Vagina
Cancer-cute (Avant Punk Army Exclusive)
War Slut
Sausagey Santa
Ugly Heaven, Beautiful Hell (with Jeffrey Thomas)
Adolf in Wonderland
Ultra Fuckers
Cybernetrix
The Egg Man
Apeshit
The Faggiest Vampire
The Cannibals of Candyland
Warrior Wolf Women of the Wasteland
The Kobold Wizard's Dildo of Enlightenment +2
Zombies and Shit
Crab Town
The Morbidly Obese Ninja
Barbarian Beast Bitches of the Badlands

FANTASTIC
ORGY

CARLTON MELLICK III

Eraserhead Press
Portland, OR

ERASERHEAD PRESS
205 NE BRYANT
PORTLAND, OR 97211

WWW.ERASERHEADPRESS.COM

ISBN: 1-936383-80-2

CONTENTS

CANDY-COATED

Knob Tyler thinks he's the strongest, toughest, most badass motherfucker on Mill Avenue. Unfortunately, Knob has a lollipop for a head. This makes him not quite as badass as he thinks he is.

While he's strutting down the street with his white muscle shirt tossed over his sweat-drenched shoulder, Knob likes to flex his pectorals at the ladies. Whenever he says *ladies*, he pronounces it *laydaaays*. But for some reason the laydaaays are never impressed by the size of his pecs. They are too creeped out by his weird lollipop head to notice anything special about his muscles. Knob's lollipop head is the size of a bowling ball and light orange in color. The flavor of the lollipop is Tropical Sensation, which is a mixture of pineapple, mango, and star fruit. His tiny candy eyes, nose, and mouth are clustered together in the center of his large round face. His eyebrows are always curled downward to show how fucking serious he is about shit.

Oftentimes, when the sun is shining hard on Mill Avenue, Knob's lollipop head will begin to sweat, filling the air with tropical sweetness. This smell attracts flies that stick to the side of his face and squirm around his ear holes. Knob tries to wipe them away, but for every fly he frees, three more take its place. This isn't good for picking up the laydaaays.

What also isn't good for picking them up is the gang of bearded truckers that always follow him around, trying to lick his head. It isn't easy to pick up laydaaays when there are bearded truckers licking your head.

But you have to understand, truckers really love Tropical Sensation-flavored lollipops. They are addicted to them.

There's something about driving a big rig down the interstate, listening to "Kansas City Lights," and sucking a Tropical Sensation lollipop down to the gooey paper stick that really makes them feel at peace with the universe. Now that Tropical Sensation is a discontinued flavor, these truckers can't do this anymore. The only way they can satisfy their tropical fix is to go down to Mill Avenue, sneak up behind Knob Tyler, and lick the back of his bald candy head.

But even this is becoming a limited resource for their Tropical Sensation needs. There is only so much licking a lollipop can take. Knob has not realized any difference while flexing in front of his mirror each morning. He is too busy watching the size of his muscles increase to notice the size of his head decreasing.

The truckers, on the other hand, have noticed the difference in size as of late. And the thought that his head might shrink away to nothing has sent a wave of panic through the trucker community.

Knob is a connoisseur of fine cheeses. Today, he is at a cheese tasting at the fancy cheesery on Mill Avenue. He holds a tiny chunk of Raclette Poivre on a toothpick, nibbling the edges with his sticky orange lips.

The shop is filled with cheese enthusiasts, gathering together for the weekly tasting. Knob struts by goateed men in gray business-casual attire, sizes them up, then moves on. Knob knows that he's the buffest cheese taster in the room. He thinks this will give him an advantage over the competition when picking up the laydaaays.

While cruising the cheesery, Knob realizes that most of the women in the room are with other guys. But this doesn't stop him from flirting at a distance. He goes to a turtleneck-sweatered woman speaking to a shrimpy, goateed man. Standing behind the man's shoulder, Knob flexes a single pectoral muscle at the woman as if it is asking her a question.

The woman knows Knob is there but she does not make eye contact, so he raises his pec even higher, then higher. The woman does not acknowledge him. He blames it on the cheesery's absurd no-shirt, no-service policy. He knows she would be much more impressed if he didn't have his shirt on.

Knob gets himself a glass of Nebbiolo and samples a Piave Vecchio. He smiles and bobs his head at the taste.

"This is a good cheese," he says to a woman breast-feeding a baby in a sling. Then he looks down at her bare breast and raises a candy eyebrow. The woman covers the baby's head and steps away.

Knob shrugs and moves on.

After five more failed attempts, Knob decides to focus on the cheeses. He has an extra-aged Mimolette, which he learns goes very well with a Zinfandel or Syrah. He then tries the Emmenthaler, which has hints of flowers, raisins, and wood fires.

"You *have* to try the Banon," says a voice behind his shoulder.

Knob turns around to see a woman with short blonde hair, square glasses, and a baseball cap. He recognizes her from previous tastings. She's one of the few regulars he hasn't had the chance to hit on yet, because she's always watching old Flash Gordon serials on her iPhone and never seems aware of her surroundings. He's checked her out, of course, and thought she was quite the hottie but a little too flat-chested for his taste (only a B-cup).

"It was aged in a chestnut leaf," she says, biting into a piece of cheese on a water cracker.

Knob looks to see if there is anybody standing behind him, just in case she might be talking to somebody else. There isn't. He raises one shoulder and slowly flexes a pectoral muscle.

"Try it," she says, pointing her cheese in his face.

Knob opens his mouth. She drops in the cheese. He chews and swallows.

"It's good," he says, his throat crusty with powdered cracker.

"I see you in here all the time," she says. "Are you really into gourmet cheeses?"

He nods his lollipop head.

"I live for cheese," she says.

"Yeah, me too," he says, his pectoral muscles dancing for her.

They turn back to the cheese table. Knob checks out the girl while she examines the cheeses. Her purple skirt wiggles when she spreads a Brie de Nangis on a slice of crusty bread. He leans in to get a better look at her front, when something wets the back of his head.

Knob turns around. There is a beefy, tattooed, potbellied trucker standing behind him holding up a piece of Port-Salut on a toothpick. Knob glares at him.

"What?" says the trucker, licking his lips through a wiry gray beard.

Knob turns back to the girl. Of all the times to have a trucker licking his head, this is the worst.

"I'm Alisa," says the girl, grabbing his hand to shake.

With his free hand, Knob feels the wet spot on his head and pulls away a few curly gray hairs.

"Knobert Tyler," he says, and bows slightly at her.

While leaning down for the bow, Knob feels two more licks on his head. He turns around. There are two more truckers behind him. These two are fatter and hairier than the first. They smile at him, holding glasses of wine and chewing on cheeses.

Knob sizes up the truckers. The truckers size up Knob. Before they get a chance to confront him, Knob turns to Alisa. He isn't sure if Alisa witnessed the truckers licking him, so he decides to play it off as if nothing happened.

"Try this Stilton," Alisa says, holding a bite of cheese to his face.

Knob opens his mouth. As he bites into the cheese, he feels wide tongues lapping at the back of his head. They squirm against his candy scalp like fat greasy snakes.

While the truckers lick his head, Knob pretends that nothing is wrong. This is his first big chance at scoring in a long time and he doesn't want to mess it up. He chews the cheese and nods at the flavor, as the bearded truckers slobber all over him.

"It tastes like ginger," he says, cringing at the curly hairs that caress the back of his neck.

"Yeah, it has mango and ginger," Alisa says.

Knob doesn't know why Alisa hasn't noticed the truckers yet. He just plays it off cool, hoping that his dancing pectoral muscles have hypnotized her. Many of the other cheese tasters have noticed the licking truckers, however, and are now politely inching away from him. Knob flexes his muscles as tightly as he can, to prove to them that he is not gay no matter how many truckers are licking his head.

"They had a five-year Gouda here last time that was really good," he says, as a warm wetness coils into his right ear hole.

Knob casually breaks away from the worming tongues and switches to the other side of Alisa.

"Yeah, yeah," she says, blinking her blue eyes. "That was terrific. I bought some to take home."

Knob feels another lick, and he turns around. The number of customers in the cheesery has suddenly doubled. Over half of them are overweight truckers who have sneaked in under Knob's radar like stealthy obese ninjas. They are spread throughout the shop, mingling with the other cheese enthusiasts. Knob can see them ogling him from across the room, winking at him between sips of chardonnay.

"They always have the most interesting cheeses at this place," Alisa says.

When she turns her back to grab some more wine, a dozen truckers charge the back of Knob's head. They hold him by the shoulders and take turns slurping on him as hard as they can. Knob tenses up like he just hopped into a freezing-cold shower. He retains a manly posture while being gang-licked by the truckers, so that none of the laydaaays watching think he's gay.

The truckers stop licking once Alisa returns to Knob. She notices that his orange head is soaked and his muscles are tensed.

"What happened to you?" she asks.

Knob slicks his hand across his lollipop head, collecting a mass of orange slime. Alisa examines his head.

"What's this?" she says, wiping her finger across a tender spot on the back of his lollipop.

Knob feels the area her finger wiped. There is a lump.

"It looks like... bone," she says.

Knob can feel it. His lollipop head has been licked down so far that it has finally degraded to the bone.

"It's your skull," she says. "Your skull is showing."

The truckers notice the white lump sticking out of the orange candy like the Tootsie of a half-eaten Tootsie Roll Pop. They bow their heads in shame. Knob fingers his head frantically, wondering what has happened to the rest of it. The other cheese enthusiasts wince at the sight of him.

"We need to get you to the hospital," Alisa says.

She sits him down in a chair. As his head lowers to her level, she gets a whiff of pineapple, mango, and star fruit.

"That smell..." She suddenly forgets about the hospital and becomes lost in the fragrance.

Then she licks his head.

"Is this..." She licks again. "Tropical Sensation?" Before Knob has a chance to ask her what she's doing, Alisa takes a few more licks and then bites down on his skull, cracking open the bone.

"I'm sorry," she says, wiping orange sauce from her lips. "I've never been able to stop myself from biting."

Everyone in the shop freezes. Yuppies and truckers

alike have their eyes locked on Knob and Alisa, their mouths drooped in horror at Knob's cracked-open skull. Unlike his lollipop head, Knob's brain looks the same as any normal person's brain, only it sweats a deep mahogany fluid that resembles a tawny port.

The taste of this brain fluid mingles with the tropical flavor in Alisa's mouth. Her eyes become distant as she rolls the mahogany liquid across her palate. Then she swallows slowly and smiles.

Knob's pecs cower toward his armpits. He holds back the pain as best as he can so that nobody thinks he's a wimp. But the crowd is no longer paying attention to Knob. Their eyes are glued on Alisa.

"Wow," she says. "It tastes even better on the inside."

Alisa takes another lick of Knob's brain, slower, really trying to get a good taste. She savors the fluid in her mouth, exploring the complexities.

She explains what she is tasting to the crowd: "It's nutty... and sweet. I can taste hints of vanilla... raisins... tobacco... strawberry..."

Then she stabs a piece of cheese with a toothpick and puts it in her mouth. Her eyes roll in euphoric bliss. "And it's just *amazing* with this Stilton."

Knob gawks at the crazy woman, wondering what is wrong with her, but the rest of the cheese tasters now seem more curious than shocked.

"You *have* to try it," she says to the cheese tasters.

The manager of the shop nudges his way through the crowd to them. Alisa arches the back of Knob's head toward the manager's nicely manicured goatee. The man dabs his tongue quickly against Knob's brain, catching only a drop of the fluid. Alisa pops a piece of Stilton through his lips and the man bites down. His eyes light up.

"Oh, my..." says the manager. "Yes, yes." He waves his wife over to Knob's head. "It is fantastic!"

After the man's wife gives it a try, she says, "This is divine!"

Knob becomes the hit of the cheesery and a hit with the laydaaays. Everyone wants to take a lick at Knob's brain, especially the truckers. They start a line that winds through the entire shop and stretches out the door.

There is not a woman in the room who doesn't want to lick him. The turtleneck-sweatered yuppie girl who had ignored him earlier slips her phone number into his pocket when her goateed boyfriend isn't looking. Knob just nods his head and pumps his pectoral muscles to the rhythm of "Kansas City Lights." The truckers raise their wineglasses in approval.

Alisa wraps her arm around Knob's neck and kisses his hard candy cheek.

"Why don't we grab a bottle of wine and go back to my place?" she says.

Knob gives her a wink. Then she cuts through the crowd to the wine section to find something special for them.

"Score," he says to himself, as the truckers and the cheese enthusiasts break off more of his candy-coating to get to the tastier flavor within.

EAR
CAT

Irene's fingers are wiggly today. They curl in and out of her hand like she is trying to snap all of her fingers at the same time.

"Quit it with the fingers already," Martin says over the videophone.

Irene paces the living room, straightening pictures of her dead parents on the coffee table, wiggling her fingers, and avoiding the pile of cats in the corner.

"Please," Martin says. "I need you."

Irene stops in front of the videophone, but she avoids looking into the screen to Martin's house. The room he's in might be dimly lit, decorated with calming earth tones, but it is still too unsettling for her. She faces his video image, but her eyes are locked on a red clay lamp directly above the monitor.

"What if it got lost in the mail?" Irene says.

"I'm sure it will come," he says. "Be patient."

Irene has been a member of the Kitty of the Month Club for over six years, and never once has a kitten been delivered this late. Her monthly kitty is the only thing that ever truly calms her down, and it has been several days since the last one expired.

"I can't be patient without it," she says.

"You're making me nervous," he says. "Calm down."

Irene realizes her fingers are wiggling, so she clenches them into fists until her knuckles go white. Then she decides to reorganize her antique lamp collection.

"Not the lamps again," Martin groans. "You just rearranged them this morning."

Irene's lamp collection covers every free inch of wall in her living room. Shelves of antique lamps start at the floor and go all the way up to the top of the seventeen-foot-high ceiling, only leaving free space for windows, a couple of couches, the front door, and the fireplace.

Each lamp is a unique work of art. There is a purple mushroom-shaped lamp, a blue porcelain lamp with sparrows painted on the side, a marble lamp shaped like a fat little German boy, a wooden withered tree-shaped lamp, a frog lamp, a shoe lamp, a fishbowl lamp. There are so many varieties of lamps clashing chaotically on her shelves that they are dizzying to the eye; the fact that she absolutely must keep every single lamp turned on at all hours of every day only amplifies this effect.

Martin sneers at Irene's lamp collection. "Why do you even bother organizing them? They look ugly no matter what order you put them in."

Irene pulls lamps off the shelves and places them on the floor. A seahorse lamp, a rainbow lamp, a child's teddy bear lamp. She keeps them all plugged in as she moves them. She can't handle to see any of them turned off, even for a minute.

"Last time they were organized by their monetary value, from most expensive to least expensive," Irene says. "Now I want to organize them by their size from biggest to smallest."

"But they're all the same size," Martin says.

Irene holds a zebra-striped lamp up to a white slinky-shaped lamp. "This one is at least an inch and a half taller than this one."

Martin groans and turns off the visual on his videophone.

"What did you do that for?" she asks the blank screen where the image of Martin used to be.

His voice comes out of the speakers on the side of the monitor. "Sorry, I can't take it anymore. Everything's so *busy* at your house."

"But you're supposed to be helping me," she says.

"And you're supposed to be helping *me*," he says. "But

all you do is make me nervous."

She wiggles her fingers at the black screen. "But we had only twenty minutes left to go. Now Dr. Ash is going to make us do it all over again tomorrow."

"I'm sorry," he says. "I hate redoing these phone sessions as much as you do, but you drove me to it."

"Fine," she says.

Irene shifts her weight back and forth in front of the screen for a few minutes. Martin remains quiet.

"Well, we might as well just cancel our conversation for the day," she says. "If we have to redo it again tomorrow, there's no point in talking anymore today."

"Sounds good," Martin says.

He disconnects before she has a chance to say goodbye.

Irene pinches the chunk of skin above the bridge of her nose. A lot of tension builds up in this area of her face, so pinching it often relieves a bit of stress. She calls this area of her face her *tickle*, because it often tickles if she goes without pinching it for too long.

She holds her tickle, her facial muscles slowly relaxing, as she sways toward her collection of previous Kitties of the Month piled sloppily on the brown-checkered carpeting.

Although the cats were once living, they are now more like stuffed animals. Gen-cats always revert to stuffed animals immediately upon expiration; their innards expel themselves out of various orifices and can be filled with cotton fluff. That's the way they were designed.

Irene picks up an ex-cat with red and tan swirls, and snuggles it against her chin. It was last January's kitty, which they called a *cinnamon cat*. Remembering back to that time, the cinnamon cat was a frisky playful kitten that freshened her house with a nice cinnamon smell all month long.

Each kitten in the Kitty of the Month Club is bio-engineered by scientists that are referred to as Kitty Artists. Their job is to invent new varieties of cats. So far, Irene has received an orange basketball kitty that bounced when it hit the ground, a unicorn kitty that had a long horn growing from its white forehead, a plushy kitty that was like an animated cat-shaped plush toy, a raspberry blue kitty, an avocado kitty, a circus clown kitty, a helicopter kitty.

They seem to have an endless variety of bio-engineered cats. So far, Irene has loved every single one of them. And once dead, they have all made great additions to her stuffed animal collection.

Normally, Irene keeps her stuffed kitties displayed on shelves in her bedroom, but whenever she is feeling lonely she likes to take them all downstairs and pile them in the living room. That way, they can be at-hand just in case she needs comfort from them.

The Kitty of the Month Club has a motto:
Comforting, High-Quality Companions, Guaranteed.

Dr. Ash refuses to call Irene on the videophone during their therapy sessions. He always insists on seeing her in person. Irene never lets him inside, so he speaks to her through a crack in the doorway. When they speak, she holds a limp goldilocks cat in her arms, with her back to the door. She doesn't want to catch even the smallest glimpse of the miserable world outside, which looks more like a long-abandoned construction site than a neighborhood street.

"You have been avoiding again," Dr. Ash says with a miniature smile. "The more you avoid, the harder it will be to confront."

Irene sticks her finger in her nose. She hates Dr. Ash. She hates that he is only twenty-two and thinks he knows everything just because he's part of the 3.5 percent of the population that isn't agoraphobic.

"I want a different therapy partner," Irene says.

Dr. Ash rubs out the wrinkles in his electric blue suit. "What's wrong with Martin?" he says.

"He's impossible," she says.

"You said that about your last eleven therapy partners," he says.

"I'm sick of seeing him on my phone," she says. "I'm sick of talking about stupid things with stupid people just because you think it will help me."

"It will help you," Dr. Ash says.

His eyebrows tighten to his eyelids to show her how genuinely concerned he is.

"What if I don't want to be helped?" Irene strokes the long golden locks hanging from the stuffed kitten on her lap.

"Don't you?" Dr. Ash says. "Don't you want to be able to go outside again?"

Dr. Ash flips through pages in a notebook. "Don't you want to go to the beach? Go out with friends? Travel to other cities, to other countries?"

She hugs the cat to her chest with all her strength. Then she pinches her tickle.

"No," she says. "I don't need any of that. What's the point in going out anymore? I've got everything I need right here. If I've got to talk to anybody, I've got email. When it's time to go to work, I log online. If I need to buy something, I shop at an online store and have it delivered. If I want to see anything interesting, the internet has millions of pictures of places that a single person could never visit in a lifetime."

"Doesn't that sound like you're just making excuses?" says Dr. Ash. "I've got dozens of other patients who say exactly the same thing."

"Whatever," Irene says, stretching her fingers out as far as she can until they begin to hurt.

"I'm going to keep you with Martin," says Dr. Ash. "I want you to stick with the same therapy partner for at least three months. The more you talk to him the more comfortable you will feel around him. Just stick with it and stop avoiding. It will get easier."

"I don't want to talk to him anymore this week," she says. "At least not until I get this month's cat."

"I want you to talk to him tomorrow afternoon for two hours," he says. "Even without the cat."

"But I can't think straight without one."

"The cat doesn't matter," he says.

"But you're the one who said I should get a pet," she says.

"I said you should get a pet," he says. "There's a big difference between getting a pet and signing up for the Kitty of the Month Club."

"What difference is that?"

"Just stop worrying about the cat," he says. "I'm sure it will come later in the day."

"It better come," she says, wiggling her fingers.

Irene logs onto the Kitty of the Month Club website to see if there is any mention of a delay in shipping this month. The front page of the site has the Kitty of the Month logo in sparkling glitter letters with cartoon kitties hopping and dancing to accordion music.

The site hasn't been updated in over a week. The This Month's Selection page is still an advertisement for last month's kitten, which was a Cheshire Kitty based on the cat from Alice in Wonderland, complete with a wide toothy grin.

After clicking on all the different pages, even checking the message board for recent announcement posts, Irene gives up. There is no mention of a delay. There is no information on what the new cat is going to be like. She begins to wonder if the company has gone out of business.

"What if there aren't any more coming?" she says to

her lamp collection. "What if I'll never get another one?"

She tries not to think about it and goes to a different website that sells brass instruments. Irene is a collector of horns. Hanging on the wall in her cellar, she has a fine collection of French horns, Vienna horns, double horns, and other brass instruments that Irene likes to call *curly horns*.

Although Irene has no idea how to play any of the instruments she owns, she likes to try. All that ever comes out when she plays are loud obnoxious noises, but there is something she finds relaxing about feeling her lips vibrate against a mouthpiece. It's not really playing the instruments that appeals to Irene. She just likes the look of her collection on the wall.

Irene loves collecting things. She has her horn collection, her lamp collection, her cat collection; these things are important to her. They are the only friends she needs.

Since she hasn't gotten her Kitty of the Month selection, Irene decides to order a new French horn. She pays to have it shipped overnight. If she doesn't get her Kitty of the Month selection, at least she will get a new horn as a kind of consolation.

The delivery machine arrives at her front door with smoke drizzling out of its faceless spherical head, its body trembling and making a loud clanking sound. Irene spies out her window at the caterpillar-shaped device as it reaches into its hollow body with rubber-coated limbs. Irene's lower lip flickers as she sees the condition of her package. The rickety delivery bot drops it out of its chest, leaving it lopsided on her doorstep. The box is wrinkled and wet, one of its sides is completely smashed inward.

"You piece of junk!" Irene yells through the door.

The machine turns around and sputters toward the next house on the gray, muddy suburban street.

Irene waits for the delivery machine to get out of sight

before making her move. As she opens the door, she focuses her eyes on the package. She steps out of the doorway with only one foot, keeping the other safely inside. Her arms stretch out to their limit and seize the edge of the package. In one jerking motion, she pulls the package inside and slams the door.

"Crappy delivery machines," Irene says, staring down at the dilapidated box.

The Kitty of the Month Club logo is scraped down to the cardboard, as if the package had been dragged across asphalt for thirty yards.

"If anything happened to it I'm going to... "

The package moves. Something is alive inside. The kitten was not destroyed during transport.

Irene smiles so wide that her lips crack. She frantically cuts the packaging tape with her front door key. It is the only thing her door key is good for anymore. While cutting, she wonders what kind of cat it will be. She thinks, will it be a rainbow-colored cat? Will it be a flying cat? Will it be a ninja cat that hides in shadows and sneak-attacks your toes when you least expect it?

When she opens the box, her smile fades away. There is something hideous inside. She's not quite sure what it is. All she can see are... ears.

The cat jumps out of the box and stretches against the carpeting, giving Irene a good look at it. The kitten doesn't have any hair. Instead of fur, the kitten has ears. It has a coat of human ears of all different sizes and shapes, sewn together in a sort of ear-kitty Frankenstein way.

Irene backs away from the cat. She isn't sure how such a monstrosity got into her Kitty of the Month Club box. She is sure that the company made a mistake. She is sure the Kitty Artists accidentally sent a failed experimental cat instead of the real one. Her hand reaches for the box. Each monthly cat comes with an introduction card explaining its unique characteristics. She is sure there will be a different cat listed on the card.

As her hand digs through the litter in the box, the thing turns its head and looks at Irene. The cat's face is like a tiny person's face, with a human's mouth, nose, and eyes.

"Meow," says the cat.

The thing doesn't meow like a cat; it says *meow* in the way that a person might say it.

Irene wonders if the thing has the intelligence of a human.

"Meow," says the cat, glaring at her with tiny blue human eyes.

The card says that it is an Ear Cat. It wasn't a mistake. This mutant animal is the right Kitty of the Month selection they sent out to everyone.

"What the hell were they thinking?" Irene says to the ear cat as it licks the lobe of an ear on its hip.

Normally, the card will give a paragraph-long story about the unique personality and physical attributes of the monthly cat, but this time all the card says is:

It has ears.

Irene's fingers are wiggly again, but this time they are wiggling faster, with more frenzied jerks. She is trying to avoid the ear cat, but the thing keeps following her around the house. She paces through the kitchen to the dining room to the entry room to the living room back to the kitchen, with the ear cat walking casually behind her. When she stops, the cat stops with her and sits down.

"Meow," says the ear cat, looking up at her with all ears raised at once as if it to listen carefully to what she has to say.

"Stop following me," she says to the ear cat, wiggling her fingers at it.

"Meow," says the ear cat.

"What do you want?" she cries.

It wags its hairless tail, which ends in a tiny baby ear

instead of a point. Irene pinches her tickle until her nerves become smooth.

The ear cat makes itself at home. It curls up onto the top of the pile of stuffed ex-cats, clawing at their fur until they become squishy and comfortable.

"No!" Irene cries at the ear cat.

The ear cat snuggles in, smearing earwax all over Irene's cat collection.

"You're ruining them!" she says.

"Meow," the ear cat whispers, its face squished against the side of a limp pirate cat.

Irene goes to her computer and visits the Kitty of the Month Club website. She is going to send them the nastiest email she has ever written in her life. On the contact page she realizes there isn't an email address. Just a phone number.

"Just a phone number?" Irene says. "I'm not going to call anyone to make a complaint."

She looks at the videophone. She knows she has been practicing phone conversations with Martin for a while, but she isn't ready to call a complete stranger. She prefers to complain by email.

During the night, Irene keeps herself locked in her bedroom. The ear cat wanders through the house. It sometimes coughs and sneezes. When it coughs, it sounds like a person coughing. It sounds like there is someone else in the house with her.

Irene lies in her bed, unable to sleep. Every time she closes her eyes and drifts halfway, she dreams there is a strange man pressing his ear against her bedroom door, trying to listen to what she is doing, and saying, "Meow."

The next day, Irene calls Martin on the videophone. Martin answers with audio only. His screen is black.

"This is a first," Martin says with a melancholy voice. "You're the one calling me."

"Turn on the video," Irene says.

"And you want me to turn the video on?" he says, trying to be witty through the quivers in his voice. "What's Dr. Ash done to you?"

Irene decides not to argue. "I'm having another panic attack."

"What is it over this time?" he says. "Did you run out of coffee again? Did one of your lamps' light bulbs burn out?"

"No," she says. "There's this strange thing in my house."

The ear cat rubs earwax against Irene's black velvet sofa.

"What kind of thing?"

"It's this cat made of ears."

"Of course."

"It was this month's kitty. It finally came and turned out to be the most horrible thing I've ever seen. It looks more like a little deformed baby than a cat."

The ear cat scratches at the wrinkles on its forehead.

"So why are you calling me about it?"

"I don't know what to do. It keeps listening to me."

"Call Dr. Ash. Ask him."

"I can't get through to him for some reason."

"Look, Irene," he says. "I'm hanging up."

"You can't hang up. You're my socialization buddy."

"I... " he says. "I don't think I want us to be socialization buddies."

"But Dr. Ash said... "

"I don't care what Dr. Ash said. Ever since I partnered with you I've become more anxious than I've ever been. I'm not going to do it anymore."

"But you can't quit."

Irene's fingers go wiggly.

"I don't care. I'm done."

"But I need your help."

"Who cares about the stupid cat?" he says. "The thing is going to die in a month anyway. Just put up with it until it dies."

"I can't put up with it," she says. "The thing is invading my home."

"Don't call me anymore. I'm disconnecting. Don't bother calling back."

The sound cuts off. Irene tries to redial his number, but he doesn't pick up.

The French horn Irene ordered arrives a day late, even though she paid for overnight shipping. The delivery machine is smoking twice as much as last time. Sparks are raining out of its abdomen. Its head is on crooked as though some kid was trying to break it off with a bat.

The box is slightly blackened on the outside, as if it had been cooking for a while within the delivery machine. At least it is not as smashed as the previous package she received.

Irene pulls out the brass instrument. Once she holds it in her hand, she realizes that it's not doing anything for her. It's not making her instantly happy the way she normally feels when she adds something new to one of her collections. It seems like just another horn. Nothing special.

She takes it into the living room. The ear cat sits down by her feet and says, "Meow." She inches away from it. It inches toward her, glaring with a frowny little man face.

Irene turns her back to the cat. She can't handle the sight of the thing, but it just leaps up onto one of the lamp shelves so that she is forced to look at it.

"Meow," says the ear cat.

Irene looks down at the French horn. It didn't make her happy to get it in the mail, but if she plays it she'll at least be able to get that vibrating mouth feeling that relaxes her.

Sucking in a large breath of air and then blowing into the mouthpiece, Irene hits one of the loudest, most obnoxious notes she has ever played.

When the ear cat hears the noise, its face cringes up. All of its ears tense up at the same time and its claws dig into the shelf. Then it flees. It charges through Irene's antique lamp collection, knocking them off the shelves. The shelf collapses, knocking down the shelf below. Like dominoes, all her shelves of rare and unusual lamps come crashing down around her.

Irene's eyes bulge open as she sees her precious collection shattering to pieces. In the center of the destruction, the ear cat licks at its wounded ears. Irene tosses her new French horn into the mess. She throws herself back into a chair, exhausted.

"That's it," she says to the ear cat. "All those years of collecting. Gone. It's ruined. I have no reason to buy another lamp, ever again."

The ear cat jumps up onto the coffee table in front of her. It cocks its head and says, "Meow."

She shudders at the little black hairs growing out of some of the ears.

Irene contemplates killing the cat. It has messed up her cat collection, ruined her lamp collection, caused her to lose interest in her horn collection. Without these collections, she has lost all her friends in the universe. The ear cat deserves to die.

She looks down at the freakish kitten. The kitten stares at her with sad raised eyebrows and pouting lips. She realizes she doesn't have the heart to kill even the ugliest of cats.

Irene opens the door a crack, without looking outside. She motions for the ear cat to go out. Although she doesn't want to kill it, she doesn't have a problem with getting rid of it.

"Come on," Irene says, snapping her fingers. "Get out."

The ear cat walks up to the door and sits down at her feet. It looks up at her and says, "Meow."

"Go on," Irene tells the ear cat.

"Meow," the ear cat tells Irene.

Then the ear cat wanders away, toward the kitchen.

Irene pinches her tickle. Before closing the door, she glances outside and contemplates leaving. It would be good to get away from the hideous creature that lives in her home. But then she reminds herself that the ear cat will not be alive for very long. She just has to wait.

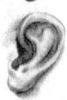

The month passes and the ear cat is still alive. It has been a long month of hiding in the bedroom, cleaning earwax off her clothes, and cringing whenever the cat coughed or cleared its throat.

She has never had a Gen-cat last so long. Normally they expire after three weeks. Sometimes two. On a couple occasions they last most of the month, but there has never been a cat that has lasted long enough to see the next month's cat.

Several days late, the smoking delivery machine crawls like a snail up the muddy street and spits out the Kitty of the Month package onto the faded welcome mat.

When Irene opens the box, her eyes tremble at the sight of the new kitten. She pulls the introduction card out of the box.

It says:

Muscle Cat—He's got muscles.

Like the ear cat, the muscle cat has a mostly human face and no fur on its body. However, the muscle cat does have hair on its head, blond hair with a surfer-style haircut. Its four limbs look like small human arms, with human hands instead of paws. These arms are incredibly muscular, as if the cat were a professional bodybuilder. The muscle cat also wears a tiny pair of purple spandex shorts.

"Meee-ow," says the muscle cat to Irene, as it flexes its muscles and flicks its blond bangs out of its blue eyes.

Irene inches away from it.

The ear cat and the muscle cat become fast friends. They play together in Irene's living room while Irene hides in her bedroom, watching them through a crack in the door.

The muscle cat bench-presses a couple of the cracked lamps that had been piled on the floor. The ear cat rocks in a rocking chair, listening to the birds singing in the dead trees outside.

The muscle cat grunts as it works out.

The ear cat coughs and clears its throat.

Irene tries to pinch her tickle to make the stress go away, but it doesn't seem to work anymore.

Irene calls Dr. Ash. He answers his videophone with the video off. She wants to see him. She thinks seeing him would make her feel more comfortable, more safe. It is the first time she has needed the company of another person.

"Irene?" he says as he answers, surprised to hear from her.

She wants to ask him to turn the video on, but can't get herself to ask the question. She hopes he will decide to turn it on himself. She waits for him to.

"Irene, I'm really busy, what do you want?" he asks.

"I need help," she says. "I can't breathe in this house. I'm drowning. I need to get out."

"Need to get out?" he says. "I thought it was the outside that made you feel like you were drowning?"

"Did you get my emails?"

"You said something about a Gen-cat that disturbed you?" he says. "You said it didn't die after a month?"

"No, it didn't," she says. "There's two of them now! The second one makes me even more uncomfortable than the first!"

"Why don't you just throw them away or kick them outside?" he asks. "They're only Gen-cats."

"I'm not touching those things," she says. "You have to come over and take them away."

She hears him exhale severely.

"Irene," he says. "I don't know how to tell you this, but I'm no longer able to be your counselor."

"What do you mean?"

"People are becoming more and more agoraphobic every day," he says. "Fifteen months ago, 94% of the population was considered severely agoraphobic. Just a few months ago, it jumped by two percent. Last month, it jumped up another two percent. Our civilization can't function with everyone locked up in their homes. We have to get outside and put the world back together."

"Then why are you dumping me as your patient?" she asks. "Especially at a time like this."

"Because I've been told to dump the hopeless cases and focus only on the ones with the best chance for recovery."

"But I'm not a hopeless case," she says.

"I'm sorry," Dr. Ash says. "Unfortunately, I really don't

have time to discuss this anymore. I have to go."

"You can't do this to me," she says.

"Good luck, Irene," he says to her.

The phone disconnects.

Her internet stops working. She isn't sure what's wrong with it. She doesn't know what to do. Everything is connected through the internet: her television, her video-phone, her job. She has become completely disconnected from the rest of the world. It is just her, the two freakish cat-things, and her wiggly fingers.

"Meee-ow," says the muscle cat, flexing its arms as it does pull-ups from a curtain rod.

She tries to ignore them, but they won't leave her alone. They follow her, meowing at her, as though they are trying to communicate.

Sitting at her computer, her twitching fingers tap on the mouse button. If she can't log online soon she could lose her accounting job. There are so many people who need online jobs and so few jobs available that she could easily be replaced within a day. Her employers have no personal connection to her. They have never met her in person nor have they even heard her voice, so they would feel no guilt in getting rid of her.

Muscle Cat strikes a pose at Irene, flexing for her. She tries not to make eye contact. Muscle Cat takes the keyboard from her lap and bends it in half, then proudly hands it back to her.

Irene glares at the mutant animal. She holds the L-shaped keyboard with three fingers, trying not to get ear-wax on her hand.

"Meow," says the muscle cat, striking another pose.

Irene looks at the door. If she could go to a neighbor's house, she could see if their internet is working and perhaps order a repairman to come out to help her. She hasn't met or seen any of her neighbors, but she assumes other people live in the surrounding houses.

She crosses the room and puts her hand on the door, but she cannot get herself to open it. She convinces herself that the neighbors have surely lost their internet connection as well, so there's no reason to bother them. She convinces herself that the internet will come back very soon.

Another month goes by and the internet still hasn't come back. Every day, Irene looks at her front door and contemplates leaving, but she always finds a reason to keep it closed.

Both cats are still alive without any sign of expiration. In their final days, Gen-cats usually grow thin and don't move around so much, but her freakish cats are as frisky as ever.

One morning, Irene finds the delivery machine collapsed outside her front door. In one of its rubber hands is another package from the Kitty of the Month Club. Irene doesn't want to open it. She doesn't want any more creepy cats walking around her house.

She takes the box inside. The muscle cat and the ear cat sit in front of it, curious about the contents within.

The box moves.

"Maybe this one will be different," she says.

When she opens it, a tiny man pops out. He is two feet tall and wears a gray business suit, a black bowtie, and a matching derby on his head. Tiny spectacles perch on the end of his nose, as he brushes a dark curly mustache with a tiny mustache comb.

Irene grabs the introduction card and steps away from the box.

It reads:

Gentleman Cat.

That is all. It is not even accompanied by a tiny description.

"But it looks like a man," she says to the card. "It doesn't look anything like a cat."

The gentleman cat walks over to Irene and bows to her. It holds out its little hand. She shakes its hand.

"Meow," says the gentleman cat, in a very sophisticated British accent.

"Meow... " Irene finds herself saying.

The gentleman cat sits on her couch, drinking tea and eating orange cranberry scones. After it takes a bite of scone, it wiggles the crumbs out of its mustache.

Irene stays far away from him. She is positive that this one isn't even a cat. It is a man. A very, very small man. She isn't sure why it is eating. Gen-cats don't need to eat. They live on protein stored in their flesh cells that lasts them long enough to survive their month-long lifespan.

She worries about him eating her food. Now that she can't order groceries, she has to survive on what she has until the internet comes back.

Gentleman Cat notices Irene glaring at the scones on his plate and tips his hat to her.

The internet doesn't come back and the food is running low. Irene tries to conserve her food, but Gentleman Cat does not understand conservation. He likes to make extravagant four-course meals for her, and prepares enough food for a family of seven.

Every morning, Irene awakes to breakfast in bed. Gentleman Cat places a tray on her nightstand and reveals the delicious meal as if revealing his latest masterpiece. Salmon benedicts, sausages, soft-boiled eggs, dried fruits, a variety of toasts, juices, and jams are all artistically arranged on the serving platter.

If Irene does not wake before breakfast is served, Gentleman Cat will stare down on her face and wake her with gentle breaths from his miniature nostrils. As soon as she begins her breakfast, Gentleman Cat will bow at her, and say, "Meow."

She knows the food isn't going to last if he keeps up this way, but she does admit to herself that the food is the best she has tasted in years.

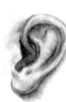

One day, Irene goes into her living room. The muscle cat is doing pushups on the floor. The gentleman cat is playing a miniature violin as the ear cat sways to the romantic melody.

The cabinets are bare. Irene hasn't had anything but tap water in a week, and though her intense hunger has faded she has become tired and light-headed from the fast. She doesn't even know how long she will have tap water to drink. Although a human can live quite a long time without food, they can't go very long without water.

She looks at the front door. She thinks about opening it, but she just can't.

Instead, Irene leans against a wall and slides to the floor. She knows she doesn't have a choice, she has to leave, but the anxiety she feels when she goes outside can be so overwhelming that she almost prefers death.

"Why am I so weak?" Irene yells at the ear cat by her foot. "I wish I was one of the strong ones."

Gentleman Cat continues to play the violin, while Muscle Cat strikes a pose.

"Do you know how great the job market is for people who aren't agoraphobic? I could get three times the amount of pay by doing half the work. But I'm weak. My mother was weak. My father was weak. They were both agoraphobic, too, back when it was still pretty rare. When I was a kid, my mother wouldn't let any of my friends come over. She was uncomfortable with the idea of strangers in her house, even kids. She also wouldn't let me go over to my friends' houses because she was too scared to drive me. I was lucky that the school was within walking distance or she would have had me homeschooled and I never would have had any friends at all."

The ear cat sits there, listening to her through all of its ears.

"Of course, I was homeschooled eventually. When I was in 6th grade, a car hit me on the way home from school. I was rushed to the emergency room with two broken legs and a concussion. My mother never came for me. She was too paranoid to leave the house. My dad came, but only to drive me home once the doctors were done with me. Then my parents never let me leave the house again. They were afraid I would get hurt again somewhere and they wouldn't be able to come help me. They wanted me to stay home, where it was safe."

The ear cat cuddles against her hand. She doesn't even realize the earwax greasing across her fingers when she pets its back.

Irene stands up and stares at the door again.

She's got to go through it. If she doesn't leave the house she's going to starve to death. She might have the worst panic attack of her life, but a panic attack is not going to kill her.

The gentleman cat stops playing his violin as Irene's hand wraps around the doorknob.

"Meow?" the ear cat says, looking up at Irene from the floor.

The door opens.

The withered, muddy neighborhood has been a frightening two-dimensional painting to her for the past ten years. She thought she would never have to enter that painting again.

She takes one step and closes her eyes. Then she takes

another. Her fingers start wiggling. At first, they wiggle slowly. After she takes another step, her wiggly fingers become frantic.

The gentleman cat steps outside and stops Irene's fingers from wiggling. He holds her hand in his tiny warm palms. She looks down at him and he bows to her. She takes another step. The gentleman cat stays with her, holding her hand as firmly as he can.

The ear cat and the muscle cat come outside with them. She takes another step. Then another. The painting of the neighborhood becomes three-dimensional. She is inside of it. It is a dizzy swirling of colors. It overwhelms her so much that she can hardly feel her body from the neck down, as if her head is floating.

When she gets to the edge of her driveway, she keeps going. She walks through the withered neighborhood. The street looks as if it hasn't been used in decades. Weeds have broken through the asphalt and overtaken the road, the sidewalks, and the walls around yards.

There aren't any more grocery stores, so she doesn't know where to go for food. Everything is delivered through the mail. All the food is hidden away in warehouses that she'll never be able to find. But she can't think about that now. She has to focus on each step. She can't let her surroundings overcome her.

There is a maple tree collapsed in the road in front of her. She stops moving. She shifts her weight from foot to foot, not sure what to do. She wants to pop her fingers, but the gentleman cat holds her hand too firmly for her to do it.

The tree rises off the ground. Underneath, Irene sees Muscle Cat. He is lifting the tree over his head as high as he can. He tosses it out of the road, into a muddy yard.

Irene nods at Muscle Cat.

The muscle cat says, "Meee-ow."

She continues on. She tries not to think too much about it. She just takes one step at a time.

Ear Cat leads the way, using his powerful sense of hearing to guide them. His body is tense. He can hear something in the distance.

Once they get closer to downtown, Irene realizes the state of what her city has become. The streets look like a tornado swept through ages ago and nobody ever bothered to clean up afterwards. The buildings are overgrown with vines, the roads have been ripped apart by roots and weeds, there are cars rusted into the sides of the street, there are piles of rubble as if bombs had gone off.

"Meow," says the ear cat, gesturing its head to the distance.

"What is it?" Irene says.

Up ahead, people are coming out of buildings. Thousands of people spill out of the surrounding apartments and houses. They climb down fire escapes, they rappel out of windows, they climb up from the sewers. All of them are confused and anxious. They look uncomfortable, fearful to be so close to each other, yet they are still drawn together. And accompanying each of these nervous people, staying close by their sides, are three cats: a gentleman cat, a muscle cat, and an ear cat.

"Meow?" says the ear cat, looking up at Irene with a wide childlike smile.

Irene nods.

She moves toward the crowds of people, taking one baby step at a time. Her head is still dizzy, her fingers are still trying to wiggle, but the three Kitties of the Month stay by her side every inch of the way.

FANTASTIC
ORGY

It was a good night for an orgy. In fact, for a single guy like me, it was the *only* night for an orgy. The Demon Seed Society only allowed single guys into the place one night a month. Women and men accompanied by women could get into the sex club any time they wanted, but not single men. If they didn't have this rule the place would always be overcrowded with a bunch of creepy-looking naked fat dudes scaring off all the ladies. But on the first Friday of every month, any guy was given a chance, no matter how fat or creepy. And boy were there a lot of creepy-looking guys in line with me that night.

Lucky for the women inside, most of these creepy guys weren't going to get in. It was the bouncer's job to weed out as many of the single men as possible. If a guy looked like he was just going to be a nuisance to the other patrons, the bouncer would tell him to take a hike. At least, that's what I read on the internet. I hadn't actually been to a swingers' sex club before.

"First timer?" the bouncer asked me once I arrived at the front of the line.

"Yeah, first time," I said, trying to look as friendly and unthreatening as possible.

I was in good shape, had nice clothes, and was not as creepy as most of the guys in line. Still, the large Ecuadorian bouncer with the bright red mustache eyed me suspiciously.

"Papers and ID," he said.

While pulling my license and STD test out of my pockets, a pack of condoms fell out onto the sidewalk.

"Those aren't allowed inside," the bouncer said, pointing at the condoms. "Not tonight."

"Sorry," I said, handing him the condoms. "I wasn't planning on using them."

The bouncer tossed the condoms aside as he flipped through my papers.

"How many STDs do you have?"

"Sorry, only one."

"Only one? It better be a good one…" he read the information about my unique sexually transmitted disease. "Dick Talk? What the hell kind of STD is Dick Talk?"

"You know … it's Dick Talk. It's exactly what you'd think it is."

The bouncer shook his head. "I don't know, bro. I don't think anyone in there wants something like that. If you had a more interesting STD, maybe…"

It was *Share Your STD Night* at the Demon Seed. Over the past few decades, sexually transmitted diseases have evolved in strange ways. Herpes, AIDS, Gonorrhea; these are all STDs of the past. These days, STDs are more extreme and bizarre. They aren't exactly diseases anymore. They are more like sexually transmitted body modifications. There's an STD that changes your hair color, an STD that causes your toes to grow larger, one causes you to grow extra breasts on your body, another causes your skin to become translucent, and there's an especially annoying STD that causes you to ejaculate miniature eyeballs. There's literally thousands of varieties, with more being discovered every day.

Many people are very careful about who they sleep with because they don't want to contract any of these strange diseases. However, some people seek out certain STDs for one reason or another. That's why I was at the Demon Seed that night. That's why most people were there.

"I've got to get in," I told the bouncer. "Just for tonight. There's an STD that I just *need*."

"Yeah, you and everyone else in this line." He waved me off. "If you don't have an STD worth getting, nobody's going to want to do you. Get lost."

"Please." I grabbed his hand and curled his fingers around two hundred dollars. "You've got to let me try."

The bouncer glanced at the bills in his hand and then discreetly stuffed them into his pocket. "Fine. Just don't cause any trouble."

He waved me over to the doorman who gave me my club badge, which had the words *Dick Talk* scribbled on the front. I paid the entrance fee and was let in.

Inside of the Demon Seed, the place was decorated with a mixture of two themes: black magic and Japanese pop music. Even though it was an adult sex club, the atmosphere seemed like it was designed for thirteen-year-old Japanese goth girls. The walls and draperies were dark purple with hints of black, with anime-style art on the walls. The images mostly consisted of busty demon girls in cosplay school uniforms. Playing in the background, there was cutesy, Japanese pop music. It was a bubbly dance song with lyrics I couldn't understand, sung by young girls with high-pitched chipmunk voices. It didn't exactly seem like the kind of music people would want to have sex to, unless they were pedophiles.

In the locker room, I ran into two large naked creepy-looking fat guys who were changing their clothing and dancing their flabby hairy asses to the Japanese school girl music. The only free locker I could find was right between them.

"It's time to get my fuck on," said the bearded fat guy.

"I ain't leavin' tonight until my balls are empty," said the bald fat guy.

These were normally the types of men the club bouncers tried to keep out, but here they were somehow. Perhaps they had also slipped the bouncer a large bribe. The two of them were breathing heavily and covered in sweat, just from the tiny amount of dancing they were doing. I couldn't imagine what state they would be in while trying to have sex.

As quickly as I could, I squeezed myself between the two fat guys and tossed my stuff into the locker. I only kept what I would wear: my club badge and my skin tight black boxer briefs, which was pretty much the only semi-sexy outfit I could think of. I thought about getting a mesh shirt to go with the boxer briefs, but I really didn't want to go into an adult boutique to buy one. These kinds of places just weren't me. I wasn't a part of this sex freak lifestyle. I just wanted to go to Demon Seed, find a woman with the STD I was looking for, contract it from her, then get the hell out of there.

Unlike myself, a lot of the Demon Seed patrons really got into their fetish fashion. The bearded fat guy standing to my left reached into his Nike duffel bag and pulled out the tiny outfit he planned to wear in the club: a leather g-string held up by studded leather suspenders. Then he strapped on a leather mask that covered all of his face but his eyes and beard. He pulled out a whip and cracked it just inches from my ass.

"Watch out, ladies," he said to himself in the mirror. "The Penetration Punisher is coming for you."

Then he stuck out his tongue and licked the chin-strap of his leather mask.

At first, I didn't think either of them had any noticeable STDs, until the bald fat guy put his hands behind his neck and jerked his hips from side-to-side.

"Wait until those bitches see the size of my fat cock," he told me.

On instinct, I looked down at his dick to see a massive misshapen appendage bouncing from thigh to thigh. His dick was like a two foot cluster of oyster mushrooms. He had one massive penis which had several miniature penises growing out of it. I looked away before the bald guy noticed I was staring, then kept my eyes inside my locker until I was ready to go.

The fat guys were actually two of the more normal-looking people in the club. Probably because nobody wanted to have sex with them, which meant they had fewer STDs than most. As soon as I stepped into the main lobby, I entered a carnival of surreal beings from alien worlds, drinking cocktails and negotiating disease trades.

There was a woman with pink polka dots covering her paper-white skin, and instead of hair she had locks of glowing blue baby arms that waved and danced above her head. There was a woman with angel wings who licked a buff dude's lollipop head. There was a young man with zebra-striped body hair and green duck feet. There was a yellow girl whose skin smoked like dry ice. There was a middle-aged woman with long wiry fingers and an upside-down face.

I scanned the crowd for some normal-looking patrons. There was only one STD I wanted. I didn't want to pick up any of the really strange ones. I didn't want to become one of *those* people. Fuck-mutants, as they were often called, were unemployable, unmarriable, and generally unwanted by the rest of society. Once you crossed the line into fuck-mutant freakdom, then that became your new way of life. You either embraced it or you locked yourself away from society for the rest of your life. I had no desire to do either.

A woman with vampire fangs turned to me, eyeing my club badge. She had four breasts sticking out of a custom-made corset. As I stepped closer, tiny red eyeballs where her nipples should be blinked flirtatiously. When I made eye contact, she opened her mouth. Three tongues poked out, coiling in seductive circles.

"Dick talk," she said.

Then she giggled. I wasn't sure if it was a playful giggle or if she was laughing at my STD. With all of the extravagant diseases in the room, mine probably did come off as pathetic and ridiculous.

When I looked at her STD badge, there were dozens of them listed. She had so many that it required multiple pages. It was more like a small booklet on a string around her neck. When I looked at the badges other people were wearing around me, I noticed many also had multi-paged STD lists. In fact, I couldn't find a single person in my area that had less than ten diseases. Surrounded by all of the strange creatures that no longer looked remotely human, I began to have second thoughts. Unless I wanted to become a fuck-mutant, I had no business being here.

"You here for some color?" asked the woman, stepping closer and spinning her tongues around clitorises that swelled between her webbed fingers.

I backed away from her. All of this was a mistake. I had to get out of there.

When I turned to leave, the two fat men from the locker room were blocking my path. They didn't let me get around them. They just marched forward, pushing me deeper into the crowd of freaks.

"Ready up them pussies, ladies," said the Penetration Punisher to no one in particular. "Get 'em hot and soggy for me."

I pushed my way through the forest of latex and wet skin, trying to get out of the fat men's way. But the fat guys followed the path I was creating, as if they thought I was creating it for them. As the bald fat guy passed the sexy she-mutants, he ogled their alien breasts, nodding and winking at each one he passed. His mushroom cluster dick bounced as he walked.

The fuck-mutants ignored the fat men. They weren't interested in them in the slightest. It was as if they were the losers of the club, even if they didn't realize it themselves. As they cruised through the crowd, the bouncers along the walls watched them carefully, as if they were used to having trouble with these two. When he was out of the bouncers' view, the Penetration Punisher put his hand up the miniskirt of a blue-skinned woman and squeezed her ass.

When she turned around, she said with five mouths, "Get the fuck off me, asshole," and slithered off.

The club had rules and one rule was that you never touched anyone without their explicit permission. The Penetration Punisher must have considered himself above such rules.

"Fuck these freak sluts," he said. "I want to fuck *clean* pussies anyway."

"I hear ya," said his bald friend.

Once I got clear of the crowd and arrived on the opposite side of the room, I was finally able to let the fat men pass me. They went through a door leading upstairs. Above the door, there was a sign that read "Pinky Lounge." *Pinkies* were what fuck-mutants called normal people, or those without too many STDs.

I decided to follow them. I hoped I would be able to find what I was looking for after all.

The disease I was looking for was called *Vibrator.* Basically, it caused your penis or your clitoris to vibrate while having sex, like a vibrator made of flesh. I wanted it for my girlfriend, Lisa, who was incredibly difficult to please in bed. She was rarely ever able to have orgasms. She always needed to use a vibrator while we made love, and even then it was pretty difficult. The only thing that really got her off was the time she had a one night stand with a guy who had the Vibrator STD. She said she came three times while having sex with him, each time more explosive than the last. She didn't even know what sex was supposed to be like before she did that guy.

I met Lisa during a work party. She was my boss's roommate and the only other person in the house who really didn't want to be there. I ran into her while I was in the kitchen and she had come out from hiding in her bedroom to make a snack.

"I hate her," Lisa said, as my boss cackled and snorted at her own lame jokes.

"You should try working for her," I said, refilling my glass with white wine.

"Trust me," she said. "I'd much rather work for her than live with her."

Then I looked down at her breasts. She was wearing a tight baby-blue t-shirt with no bra. I could see her nipples through the fabric. Her breasts pointed out so far that they lifted the bottom of her shirt up high enough to expose her belly button and her underwear sticking out the top of her jeans. I blushed when she noticed me checking her out. It seemed like she was just going to let it slide, but then I got an erection and my penis started talking.

"What's that?" she asked, looking down at my crotch.

"What? Nothing. I don't hear anything." I said this while pointing my crotch away from her.

"It's coming from your pants," she said.

Perhaps it was because I was drunk, but I decided to tell her all about my STD, which I had obtained back in college when a drunken punk chick passed out in my bed with me after a big party. Since she was my boss's roommate, telling her was a pretty stupid thing for me to do. I could have been fired if my boss found out.

"I have Dick Talk."

"What's that?"

"It's a disease," I said. "It causes me to pick up talk radio stations whenever I have an erection."

"Really? Talk radio comes out of your... "

When I caught her looking down at my penis, she was now the one who was blushing.

"It's just one particular station," I said. "I can't change it."

"What station?"

"I don't know. I try not to listen to it. Usually, it's just a bunch of ranting from right-wing extremists."

"Sounds kind of annoying," she said, as she tried to make out what the people were saying inside of my pants.

"Even more annoying is how the voices vibrate against my thigh," I said, trying to adjust my erection while turning my back to her.

Her eyes lit up when I mentioned the word *vibrate*. Then she asked me for my phone number. I didn't know why she was interested in me then, but later I discovered it was because she wanted to see if Dick Talk felt anything like Vibrator. It didn't, unfortunately, but she decided to continue dating me anyway, because she said a penis with Dick Talk was still a lot better than normal penises. She made me use condoms though, because she didn't want to contract my disease. She didn't want to hear the rants of asshole Republicans coming from her vagina all the time, even though she was a Republican herself.

After dating awhile, we eventually fell in love. We were a good couple. We both had steady jobs. We both liked the same television shows. We both wanted the same things out of life. We both loved each other's company. There was only one problem: our sex life was getting worse and worse.

The other day, when she was away from her computer, I discovered that she had signed up for an online dating site. Her ad said that she was looking for a guy who had Vibrator. I had to read it several times to be sure it was true. At first I was angry, but then I was worried. I didn't know what I would do if Lisa left me for another guy. She meant everything to me.

I knew the only way to save our relationship would be to get the Vibrator STD myself. If I was a better lover, I was sure she wouldn't leave me. That was why it was so important to go to the Demon Seed that night. I had to get Vibrator before anyone responded to her personal ad.

There weren't as many people in the Pinky Lounge as there were in the main lobby, but none of them were fuck-mutants. Most of them looked like normal human beings. There were a few people with slightly strange modifications: a guy with claw-like toenails, a girl with glowing green eyes, and a guy with peacock-colored hair. None of them had STDs that couldn't be covered up.

A large percentage of the pinkies were male who were there for one reason: they wanted the STD that would make their dicks bigger. Only one girl had the Dick Growth STD and she wasn't putting out for anything but Breast Growth.

When she saw me enter the room, the short-haired pixie-like girl ran over to me and said, "Do you have it? Please, please have it." She jumped up and down at me, pointing at my badge which had accidentally flipped over to the blank side. "I'll give you Dick Growth if you do."

When I flipped it over, her face became an exaggerated frown and she walked away. It seemed like she had been waiting all night for somebody to show up with Breast Growth.

I went to the bar and ordered a Long Island Iced Tea. I needed something strong. This just wasn't my kind of scene.

"Pace yourself," the bouncer near the bar said as the bartender mixed my drink. "If you're visibly intoxicated I have to toss you out."

I nodded at him as I paid for the drink.

When I turned back, the two fat guys were cornering the tiny blonde girl.

"Looking for bigger tits, huh?" asked the Penetration Punisher. "I'll give you bigger tits."

The girl read his STD badge, "You don't have Breast Growth."

"No," he said. "I've got something better: Math Power. Do it with me and it'll improve your math skills. Then you'll be able to get a good accounting job and make enough money to buy breast implants."

The petite girl squeezed out from between them and said, "No, thanks," as she hurried away. By the look of disgust on her face, she probably wouldn't have slept with the fat guy even if he did have Breast Growth.

I scanned the crowd for someone with Vibrator. One of the guys had it, but I didn't want to get it from him just as much as he didn't want to give it to me. As I went from girl to girl, they checked out my badge as I checked out theirs. I didn't make eye contact with any of them. They saw Dick Talk and moved on. I didn't see Vibrator so I moved on. None of the girls had what I wanted, so I did what everyone else was doing. I waited around for somebody to show up with the right disease.

It was two hours and two more drinks before a girl with Vibrator showed up. When I saw her, she gave my badge one glance and walked away from me. I tried to chase her down and beg her to give me the disease, even if I had to pay her for it, but that only pissed her off more.

The bouncer got between us. "She doesn't want your STD. Leave her alone or you're out."

I calmed myself and went back to a chair near the bar. By a strike of luck, another girl with Vibrator appeared just a few minutes later. She must have already been at the club for a while, because she was coming out of the showers, topless with a towel wrapped around her waist.

"You have Vibrator?" I asked, running into her path. I'm sure I came across as desperate, but I didn't care.

She was a cute Mexican girl. She was short, maybe four foot eleven, but she had the breasts and ass of a woman six foot two.

"You want Vibrator?" she asked, fluffing her curly black hair to the side. She didn't immediately say no or ignore me, which was a good sign.

"What do I get?" she asked.

A Popeye tattoo jiggled with her right boob.

She looked at my badge.

"Dick Talk?" She looked up at me and then back down. Then she smiled. "Holy shit. If I get that does it mean I can make my pussy talk?"

I nodded. I didn't want to explain it in more detail.

"Oh, fuck yeah, chico," she said. "It would be so fucking hot if I could talk with my pussy. I *so* want that."

Then she paused to check out my body. She licked her round juicy lips, which were naturally dark around the edges. Then her big brown eyes gazed into mine and without any words, she told me that she was going to fuck the hell out of me. When I checked out her body more thoroughly, I realized that I was about to sleep with one of the hottest girls in the club. The only thing unattractive about her was an odd lightning bolt-shaped scar on her forehead.

She grabbed me by the wrist and pulled me toward the hallway.

"What's your name?" she asked.

I didn't realize people asked for names in a club like this.

"Tim," I said, staring at her bare ass falling out of the towel as she walked in front of me.

She looked back. "Maria."

Then she kept going, not letting go of my hand until we were in one of the private bedrooms, as if I was a treasure she didn't want to let go of, didn't want anybody to snatch from her before she got her turn. But she was going to be in for a surprise once she found out what Dick Talk really did. It wasn't as if she'd be able to control what her vagina said once she got it. I didn't care about her, though. I needed to get Vibrator, no matter what it took.

Even if I had to lie about my STD and give it to a girl who really didn't want it.

As we entered an empty bedroom, I realized that I was too excited to see Vibrator that I didn't actually get a good look at any of her other STDs. Just by looking at her, she didn't seem to have anything too extreme, so it was probably okay. She shut the door, dropped her towel, and removed her badge. Then she pushed me against the wall and pulled off my boxer briefs.

On her knees, she looked up at me with hungry eyes.

"Talk to me through your dick," she said. "Say *fuck me, Maria.*"

I wasn't sure how I was going to get around this.

"I've got to be erect for it to work," I said.

She looked at my flaccid penis as if she hadn't noticed it yet.

"I'll take care of that," she said, then put her tongue on my scrotum and licked all the way up the shaft to the head. It chubbed up a little, but not enough to turn on the talk radio station.

I had to come up with a plan. As soon as I was erect I was going to take control of the situation and advance to the next stage of having sex before she figured out what words were coming out of me.

She rolled my soft member against her luscious lips, pressing her tongue against the area just beneath the edge of the penis head, trying to get it harder. Then her eyes rolled back and her forehead fell against my belly, pulling my entire dick inside of her mouth. I could feel it getting a little harder while pressed against her tongue. But she didn't move any more after that. She just went kind of limp, with her lightning-scarred forehead leaning against my stomach and my penis lying in her mouth.

I stood there awkwardly for a couple minutes, wondering what was going on with her. Then I looked over at her badge and saw that one of her STDs was called Narcolepsy. The girl was asleep.

Before trying to wake her up, I debated whether or not contracting Narcolepsy was worth it. Narcolepsy seemed even worse than Dick Talk. I looked at her badge again. She also had a disease called *Harry Potter*, which must have been the lighting bolt scar on her forehead. I didn't realize her scar was actually an STD that I could contract. I thought it was just a normal scar. When I saw the word *Popeye*, I realized that the Popeye tattoo on her breast also wasn't a regular tattoo. It was a sexually transmitted tattoo of Popeye. She also had the diseases *Toe Fetish, Wider Belly Button,* and *Puppy Fun*. The first two seemed easy to figure out, but I had no idea what the hell Puppy Fun could have been.

I was almost ready to push the girl off of me and leave the room, when she woke up and continued sucking on my flaccid penis. That's when I decided I would go through with it. For all I knew, it was my last and only chance to get Vibrator. It was worth getting all of those other diseases as long as I could keep Lisa. She was that important to me. I didn't care if I got Narcolepsy, a wider belly button, a big facial scar, and whatever the hell Puppy Fun was.

"Oh, hell yeah," Maria said, as my penis started to grow in her mouth. "Tell me you want to fuck me."

"I want to fuck you," I told her.

"Not with your mouth." She grabbed my lips with her fingers and held them closed. "I want your dick to tell me."

She sucked on my penis until it was fully erect. The second it started blaring the talk radio channel, she giggled against my shaft as the words tickled her tongue. The radio voice was muffled inside of her mouth, so she couldn't understand what was being said. It could as well been saying *fuck me, Maria* over and over again, just as she wanted.

When she pulled my penis out and stared into the hole, she laughed as the hole moved like a talking mouth. Then she listened to the words.

"I don't care if they're dying," said my penis. "American hospitals should be for American citizens."

Maria looked confused. She didn't know why I would say such a thing while we were getting down and dirty. She put my penis back in her mouth and gave me an awkward blowjob while she tried to listen to what was being said.

"Illegal aliens are stealing our healthcare every day and it needs to stop," the muffled radio voice said inside of her mouth. "If Mexicans come here illegally and die as a result of not getting healthcare in American hospitals then that is their own fault. They shouldn't be here to begin with."

She spit me out. "What the fuck?"

"Our healthcare is for Americans, not Mexicans."

"Why would you say that to me?" she asked. "Are you trying to be funny or something?"

"No, it's not me," I said.

"Fuck Mexicans," my penis-mouth told her. "There, I said it. Fuck. Mexicans. They're ruining our economy."

"Fucking asshole!"

She pushed me away from her and stood up.

"I don't have control over it," I said. "It's just a radio station."

She grabbed her things. On the way out of the room she punched me in the stomach so hard I fell to the floor.

"I'll fucking cut you if I see you again," she said, slamming the door behind her as I curled into a ball.

"Arizona's the only state headed in the right direction," my penis said beneath me. "Illegal immigration should not be tolerated. It doesn't matter how extreme the measures are, we can't afford not to take them."

I couldn't go back out there and face other people while I had this intolerant jackass ranting through my dick like a megaphone. So I just lay on the floor, waiting for my erection to fade.

When I returned to the Pinky Lounge, Maria was already taking another guy and his girlfriend into one of the private rooms. I waited in the lounge with a martini, listening to Japanese high school love songs, not too hopeful I would find another girl with Vibrator. The Penetration Punisher was still doing rounds with the women in the Pinky Lounge. He wasn't having any luck, but he kept trying. He seemed pretty confident that the women wanted to be punished with his penis, no matter how many times they rejected him. His friend was having even less luck than he was. With his grotesque oyster mushroom penis, nobody wanted to go near him. People would scatter whenever his penis came within a twenty foot radius of them, as if they might get his hideous disease just by brushing against it.

With no new women arriving and a lot of people beginning to leave, I decided to give up and go. But before I headed out, I took a walk around the club, exploring all of its secret nooks. The place was a three story labyrinth of bondage dungeons, group sex halls, porn theaters and hot tubs. The fuck-mutants seemed to enjoy being on exhibition, so many of them kept their doors wide open.

While poking my head into one of the hot tub rooms, I saw two women who looked like bug-eyed gray aliens making out with each other as a man with octopus tentacles for a penis serviced their every orifice. His tentacles were so massive that they filled the entire Jacuzzi, twisting in and out of the water like sea serpents.

"You like to watch?" asked a woman peeking into the room from over my shoulder.

I hadn't seen her there. She seemed to just appear.

"Uh... " I began.

"I like to watch," she said.

She was an abnormally tall girl, wearing sunglasses,

a t-shirt, no bra, and men's underwear. Her body was a lot like Lisa's. Her facial structure also reminded me of Lisa. In fact, everything about her reminded me of Lisa. I would have thought it was actually her if it wasn't for the woman's long blonde hair with a black stripe through it.

"Yeah," I said.

I lied so that I could ogle this woman some more. Before I met Lisa, I wouldn't have said that she was exactly my type. She wasn't unattractive or anything, though she didn't perfectly fit my previous definition of beauty either. But after I fell in love with her, it seemed that the only girls I was attracted to at all were the ones who reminded me of her in some way. This girl definitely reminded me of Lisa.

"They're so beautiful, aren't they?" the woman said. "They make love like they're dancing for us, performing a ballet."

As she stared at them, I could tell she was becoming aroused. Her body quivered with ecstasy. Her skin and t-shirt moistened with sweat, which released a kind of fruity fragrance. As I watched droplets of perspiration dribbling down her neck, I too was becoming aroused.

I jumped with shock when the talk radio came on. It was extra loud and seemed to play in stereo. The woman also jumped in shock. We both looked down at our crotches and adjusted, then we looked at each other. I realized that the radio program wasn't just coming from my pants. It was also coming from the woman's boxer shorts.

"You have Dick Talk?" the woman asked.

"Yeah." I fidgeted with my erection, but it only made it louder.

"Me too!" she said excitedly. "Err, I mean I've got Pussy Talk, or Cunt Talk, or whatever a girl would call it." She patted her pubic hair through her underwear. "Doesn't it suck?"

I laughed. "Oh yeah."

The three fuck-mutants in the hot tub gave us dirty

faces as they heard the talk radio noises. We were disturbing their moment.

"Oops, sorry," the woman said, squeezing her thighs together to muffle the voices. "We'll leave you alone."

Then she closed the door and giggled.

I found myself strolling through the hallway with the woman, peeking in at the different fuck-mutants as we went. Both of our crotches were still tuned in to the talk radio show. The subject was Jesus. We didn't speak to each other at first, but then she introduced herself.

"The name's Cory," she said, trying to speak over the noise coming from our privates. "You're a Pinky, right?"

"Tim," I said. "Yeah. Aren't you?"

"Not exactly," she said. "But I'm really low status."

"Low status?" I asked.

"Once you get out of the Pinky Lounge," she said, "this club is all about status. The people at the top of this scene are the ones with the most unique combinations of STMs."

"STMs?"

"Sexually transmitted modifications," she said. "We don't think of them as diseases here. Diseases are bad for you. What we spread to each other aren't diseases, they are improvements. We are trying to become living works of art."

"I thought the transformations were just about having crazy unusual sex?"

"Yeah, well there's that, too."

We peeked in at an S&M dungeon where a seven-foot-tall woman with antlers growing out of her head was flogging a man with bunny ears. The man was bound to the wall, thrashing to get free, frothing at the mouth. His teeth were made of what looked to be barbed wire and his eyes looked like those of a snake. Black blotches covered his naked skin like hives. As soon as they heard our crotches, the deer woman kicked the door closed with the horseshoe attached to the bottom of her hoof.

After another ten minutes of walking around, our crotches were still blaring, annoying everyone we came across.

"You still have an erection," Cory said to me.

"So do you," I said.

"I'm a girl," she said. "I don't think you're supposed to call it an erection when girls are turned on."

"I wouldn't know about that," I said.

"So I guess we're both turned on," she said. "And having a hard time turning off while we're around each other."

"Yeah," I said.

"Maybe we should do something about that," she said.

"Maybe," I said.

"What other STMs do you have?"

"Just Dick Talk," I said.

"Just Dick Talk? Serious?" She looked down the hallway for an available room. "Oh well. I won't get any mods out of it but I guess I can do you for fun. I'm dying to try out one of my new STMs I just got anyway."

Even though I couldn't get rid of my erection, I knew better than to do a girl at the Demon Seed just for fun. I was there for one reason only.

"Do you have Vibrator?" I asked. "I want Vibrator."

"Of course," she said. "Everyone has Vibrator."

"Everyone? I've been looking all night for Vibrator."

"Well, finding anything you want among Pinkies is always difficult. But everyone I know in this scene has Vibrator somewhere in their list of STMs."

"How many STMs do you have?"

"Maybe thirteen or fourteen."

"You don't look like you have that many."

A lock of her blonde hair raised from her head and wrapped around my neck like a snake. "You'd be surprised at the number of STMs some people have."

I looked at her badge and examined her list of STMs.

Most of them sounded like they would be great to have. Vibrator, Breast Growth, Penis Growth, Apricot Sweat (which made her sweat smell like apricots) and Tulip Turds (which made her shit smell like flowers). All of these seemed like they would help my relationship with Lisa even more. Hair Tentacles seemed like it could come in handy, being able to grab things with my hair. If it became a problem, I could just cut my hair short. She also had Black Stripe, which I guessed was what caused the black stripe in her blonde hair. That one wasn't a problem. I had black hair already so it wouldn't actually show up. There was only one I didn't understand.

"What is Hello Kitty Eyes?" I asked.

The woman pulled down her sunglasses and revealed two white and pink kitty faces where her pupils should be.

"My eyes are little Hello Kitty heads."

At first, I thought that disease was a bit too much for me. But then I realized that I could always get color contacts that could cover them up. It was worth the sacrifice for Lisa.

"Alright, sounds good," I said. "I'd be fine with all of those STMs."

"Are you sure?" she asked.

"Yeah," I said.

"It'll be a big step for you," she said. "It will change your life forever. Are you sure you aren't too drunk to make such a major decision?"

"I'm fine."

She held out her badge for me to read. "Are you sure? Even with the new one I just got? That one is huge. You'll never be the same again and it's irreversible."

I looked at her badge at something written at the bottom with a pen. The ink was smudgy, as if the steam from the hot tub rooms had melted it off. Even though it stretched in a blob down the card, I could still make it out. It said Double Tongue. I thought it was no big deal. Even though the girl had two tongues, she was still able to speak fine. I figured I could handle having an extra tongue. It was a pretty big modification, but easily hidden.

"I would love to have all of your STMs," I said. I wasn't more sure of anything in my life.

The way she smiled at me after I said that was as if my response was turning her on even more.

Inside of a private room, she kissed me with her new tongues. They coiled around my own tongue, trying to pin it against the side of my mouth as though we were thumb wrestling. She pushed me onto the bed and wrapped her tentacle hair around me, pulling me closer to her.

"I'm really excited for this," she said, but I could hardly hear her over our Dick and Pussy Talk.

She pulled off my boxers and wrapped her double tongues around my penis, pulling it into her mouth, quieting the Christian extremist ranting from my penis hole.

"I wish you could ejaculate this asshole out of your dick so I could bite his head off," she said.

She threw off her t-shirt and pulled down her boxer shorts.

"Are you ready to be changed forever?" she asked.

I nodded.

Her pubic hair moved on its own, spreading out to expose her vagina. The labia were moving to the voice coming out of her. Vagina Talk looked even more ridiculous than Dick Talk.

"I'm so fucking wet," she said, touching her pussy. "It feels so weird."

She put her breasts in my face and wanted me to suck on her nipples.

"Wow," she said, as I sucked them. "Oh, yeah, I like that."

She was sounding like a bad porn actress for some reason.

Then she slapped her boobs across my face one at a time and said "Boing" every time she did it. The act amused her so much she giggled. I had no idea why.

She squeezed her breasts as hard as she could and made a growling noise at me.

"My tits are so fucking hot," she said.

She was definitely right that she had great breasts, but I didn't know why she had to brag about it.

"Oh, fuck," she said as she straddled me and rubbed two fingers along her vaginal lips. "My pussy feels so fucking good. You're going to *love* it."

By the way she was talking, I surmised that she was a bit of a narcissist.

Her long hair curled around my wrists and neck, then she grabbed my penis and stuffed it inside of her. On top of me, she grabbed my shoulders and fucked me slowly, savoring every centimeter of my cock.

"Holy fuck," she said, between moans. "I didn't know it would feel like this... It's so fucking awesome."

My penis talked inside of her, as her vagina talked around my penis. Her clitoris vibrated against me and her tongues swirled against my neck. It was the first time I'd had sex without a condom in a very long time, so I was extra sensitive. I felt as though I would cum at any second, and so did she.

Cory flipped me over so that I was on top of her.

"Fuck my pussy," she said. "Fuck it hard."

I fucked her as hard and as fast as I could, but I was barely able to hold back the orgasm. She groped her breasts as I fucked her, licking one of her nipples with her double tongue.

"I want to feel you cum inside of me," she said. "It's going to feel so fucking good."

I was getting ready for orgasm.

"Cum in my pussy," she said. "Cum in me."

I could feel it coming.

"Being a woman is so fucking hot," she said.

I was ready to burst. She shoved my face between her breasts.

"When you change we need to have some hot lesbian sex," she said.

Before I could ask her what she meant by that, I came inside of her. She giggled in amazement as my dick pumped in her. It made her cum at the same time.

When we were done she lay back and said, "That was amazing. You've got to try it."

"Try what?" I asked.

"Fucking a guy once you become a woman," she said.

"What are you talking about?"

Cory looked at me in a confused way, surprised that I had no idea what she was talking about.

"Gender Swap," she said. "My new STM that I just got. The one I wanted to try out on you."

"Gender Swap?" My skin was beginning to feel tight.

"I thought you knew," she said. "It changes your gender."

"You mean I'm going to become a woman?"

"Yeah."

My eyes quivered. She had to be wrong.

"I thought your new STM was Double Tongue," I said. "I thought that was what you wanted to try out."

"That's a new one, too," she said. "But Gender Swap was written just under it."

Cory looked down at her badge and her mouth dropped open.

She said, "Oh fuck, it's smudged off."

Then she looked up at me with an apologetic face.

"Oh, dude..." she cried. "I'm so, so sorry. I didn't realize... I thought you knew."

"So I'm going to become a woman?" I asked.

I ran to a mirror. There was no change yet.

"When will it happen?" I asked. "How can I stop it?"

"You can't stop it," she said. "It's permanent." She followed me to the mirror. "It should happen pretty soon. It took ten minutes before I changed."

"Wait, you used to be a man?" I asked.

"Well, yeah," she said. "I was a guy when I came here

tonight. But don't worry, bro. It doesn't make you gay or anything. I'm one hundred percent woman now. I can get pregnant, have periods. It's as if I was born a woman."

"I could get pregnant?" I asked.

"Sure," she said. Then she looked down at her crotch. "Fuck, I guess you could have even gotten me pregnant just now. I just became a woman, so I'm not on the pill or anything."

"What?"

Then the changes happened. My eyes changed first. I blinked in the mirror and in an instant my eyes were pink. Two Hello Kitty faces were staring back at me. Then my hair started growing into long, dancing locks that looked like tentacles. My tongue split into two. The sweat pouring down my face had a strong fruity odor. Black stripes started appearing on my skin.

"What's going on?" I said, as the stripes appeared all over my body like a zebra.

"Oh shit, bro," Cory said. "You got a new mutation. The Black Stripe STM changed your skin rather than your hair. You're the first that's ever happened to."

I tried to block the stripes from my mind, too focused on when the gender change would happen.

"You're special," Cory said, rubbing her fingers along the stripes on my skin. "Everyone's going to want a piece of you now."

Then my breasts started to grow. I put my hands on them and soft mounds of tissue were swelling outward. I looked down at my cock. It grew a few inches at first, but then it started to shrink. It became smaller and smaller until it was sucked into my quivering pubic hair. I felt it. There wasn't any penis left. Just some puffy layers of skin.

My waist caved in, my hips expanded, my nipples widened, some of my upper body mass disappeared. I was a woman. As my breasts finished growing, they felt enormous on my body, even more enormous than they looked. The weight of them was awkward, kind of uncomfortable.

They were even bigger than Lisa's.

As I thought about Lisa, my Hello Kitty eyes began to shake in the mirror. How was I going to explain this to her? Lisa was as straight a woman as they possibly came. There was no way she would ever want to be with me after the sex change. She would leave me for sure. Our relationship was over. My life was over.

"I fucked up," I said to the mirror, tears running from my pink eyes.

Cory wrapped her arms around me, her breasts squished against my striped breasts.

"Don't worry, bro," she said. "You'll be okay. Look at you."

She pointed at my reflection in the mirror. A strange woman stared back at me. I didn't recognize myself. The only thing that resembled the old me was my hair color.

"You're a hot chick now," Cory said. "You'll have a sweet life from here on out."

Tears rolled down my cheeks.

"Come on, babe," Cory said. She grabbed my breasts and wrapped her hair tentacles around my hair tentacles. "Let me make you feel better."

She licked my neck and put my nipple in her mouth. It was so sensitive that it made me yelp when she sucked on it. Her hand reached between my legs and caressed my new vagina. It wasn't ready to be penetrated, so her dry squirming fingers rubbed my insides raw. I pulled away. She got on her knees and used her tongues instead.

"Don't," I told her.

"It'll be okay, baby," Cory said.

Then she bent me over and licked my new vagina from behind, shoving her nose into my ass as she curled her tongues within the folds. When the talk radio blared out of my vagina, I jumped. I stepped away from her, staring her in the eyes. All I saw in those kitty faces was a horny guy, trying to pressure a girl into sex.

"Just enjoy yourself," she said, playfully.

I stepped back toward the door.

"Where do you think you're going?" she said. Her playful voice was growing annoyed. "I changed you. That makes you mine, bitch."

I ran out of the room. Without any clothes on, I covered my new parts with my hands and ran down the hall.

Cory peeked out of the door. "Get your ass back over here, cunt."

Her voice scared me. Her tone was like that of an abusive alcoholic boyfriend. For all I knew, she could have been a complete asshole before she became a woman. She could have even been a sex offender. Either way, it didn't seem like she had been the kind of guy who would respect women. I kept running.

Cory followed me, but not very far. She saw a bouncer who almost stepped in to help me. I thought about telling the bouncer what had happened, and how I was tricked into getting an STD I didn't want. But I decided I just needed to get out of there as soon as possible.

I didn't have the key to my locker anymore, so I went to the showers to get a towel. The shower room was full of steam. I couldn't see anyone inside of there. Outside of the showers, all of the towels were soaking wet and smudged with something brown that resembled shit. But somebody had left behind some clothes, so I went for them. They were women's clothing. There was a black leather corset with red laces, latex sleeves and leggings, and a vinyl skirt. I had no idea what my clothing size was as a woman, but they seemed like they could fit.

I looked around to make sure nobody was watching. As I pulled on the latex pants, I realized how much more comfortable tight pants were without having a penis between my legs. I actually liked the way it felt against my skin. But as I put on the corset, the leather was rough against my nipples and my body felt contorted into unnatural directions. I didn't even dare try to wear the high-heeled shoes.

As I stuffed my breasts inside of the corset, I heard a moaning sound echo through the bathroom. A woman's moan. I turned to see a lone figure writhing within the steam.

She might have been the owner of the outfit I was wearing, so I decided to get out of there quickly and quietly. But while trying to sneak away, her moaning became growling, then screaming. I turned back, wondering what was wrong with her. I stepped closer to investigate. Lying on the floor of the shower room, it was a woman with calico cat fur covering her body. She was rolling around on the ground, frothing at the mouth. She was having some kind of a seizure.

"Are you all right?" I asked.

She didn't respond. She kept thrashing and rolling around. Behind her fur, I could see her skin was covered in many black hive-like splotches. Her teeth were clenched tight and looked as if she was wearing braces made of barbed wire.

I scanned the area. Nobody else was in the room. I backed out of there, wondering if I should let one of the bouncers know about her condition.

Out in the hallway, I could hear the sounds of a violent orgy going on in one of the rooms. I couldn't tell which room. It sounded like ten or twenty people fucking each other so hard they were screaming.

I couldn't find a bouncer, so I decided to just get out of there. I didn't want to stay another second. My eyes were tearing as I marched with latex-squeaking thighs down the hall. As I turned a corner, I ran into two naked fat guys. I plowed into their bellies and fell backward. When I looked up, I found myself face to face with the Penetration Punisher.

"Hey," said the fat bearded man. "Where do you think

you're going in such a hurry?"

The bald fat guy said, "You are one fine sexy bitch."

They closed in on me, backed me into a corner.

"So," said the Punisher, "you wanna get good at math?"

Then he stuck his tongue out of his leather mask at me.

The bald fat guy pointed his enormous mushroom-cluster dick at me. I felt its fluffy folds rubbing against my upper thigh. He said, "Want to ride my fat cock?"

I squeezed myself as far as I could into the corner, covering my cleavage with my hands. But no matter how far I squeezed, they kept inching in closer.

"How about a tag team?" said the Punisher. "You can have the both of us at once. I'll punish your hot steamy snatch while you titty-fuck my friend's monster dong."

I looked around the hallway for a bouncer, but there wasn't one to be seen. All I heard was screaming coming from behind closed doors as the orgy grew to a climax.

"No, thanks," I told them.

I tried pushing my way out, but the fat guys wouldn't budge. They were too much weight for me to move. And because there were no bouncers around, these two were extra aggressive.

"Come on, sexy bitch," said the bald guy. "You know you're dying for it."

The Penetration Punisher said, "Your mind might be telling you no, but I can tell your pussy's just screaming for my cock."

These guys were bad enough when I was male. Once I became a woman they were absolute nightmares. There was only one way out of this that I could think of.

"I'm not a woman," I told them.

They were confused.

"When I came in here, I was a guy," I said. "I was between you two in the locker room, remember? I trans-formed into a woman just minutes ago, when I acciden-tally got the Gender Swap STD."

The two fat guys looked at each other, then back at me.

"So you used to be a guy?" asked the Punisher.

"Yeah," I said, pushing them back a little.

They examined my body.

"But now you're a chick?" the bald guy said. "You've got a real vagina and tits and everything?"

"Yes."

The two fat guys looked at each other, then back at me. Then both of them shrugged.

"I'd still do you," said the bald fat guy.

"Yeah," said The Penetration Punisher. "As long as you're a woman now, it wouldn't make us gay. Besides, you've got some awesome tits."

"I want to rub my dick between those tits," said the bald guy.

"I want to cum on those tits until they look like two big glazed donuts."

"Dudes!" I yelled at them. "You're really creeping me out. I'm a guy. I'm not gay."

The two fat guys fell silent for a moment, then the bald guy said, "You're not a guy anymore."

"Yeah," said the Punisher. "And you've got to break that pussy in sometime."

They closed in on me again. The bald guy's grotesque penis was erect and poking into my belly.

I thought they were about to grab me and drag me into a room with them, when a fuzzy figure stumbled into the hallway. Coming from the shower room, the calico cat girl was no longer having her seizure. She was staggering toward us, blood and foam dripping down her chin. She looked incredibly drunk.

"You okay?" asked the Penetration Punisher. Then he whispered to his friend. "She looks drunk."

"Too drunk to say no, huh?" said the bald guy. I could feel his dick bouncing when he chuckled.

"Why don't you take her," the Punisher said. "And I'll take this bitch."

"But I want the big-titted bitch," said the bald guy. "You take the furry bitch."

The Punisher grabbed my shoulder. "This bitch is mine. I saw her first."

"But it's my giant cock she wants." The bald guy rubbed his fluffy, bulbous penis up my belly more. "See, she loves it."

"Fine, we'll leave it up to her," said the Punisher. He turned to me, "Which of us do you want to fuck?"

"She wants *my* cock," said the bald guy.

I pushed his monster penis away from me. "I don't want your fucking cock!"

The Punisher smiled. "See, I told you she wanted me more than you."

The bald guy gave me a dirty look and stepped away.

"Fine," said the bald guy. "I'll take the kitty cat. I like my pussies furry anyway."

He strolled over to the staggering cat woman. His penis rubbed up her furry chest as he pulled her arm around his waist. The Punisher turned to me. He put both of his hands on the wall, trapping my head between them.

"Ready to improve your math skills?" said the Punisher, licking his lips.

He went in to kiss my neck, but a scream stopped him short. We turned to his bald friend. The cat woman was like a rabid animal. She ripped the fat man's mushroom-cluster dick off with barbed wire teeth, thrashing it around in her mouth. The bald fat guy cried and tried to hold in the blood that was spraying from his crotch. Then the furry woman tore open his belly in a tornado of claw-scratches, like she was trying to dig through him.

The Penetration Punisher stepped forward. "What in the fuck!"

The woman looked up at him with cold black snake eyes. Then she grabbed his friend by the throat and pulled his limp body out of the hallway, into a room, like a jaguar trying to protect its meal from other predators. All we could see was the bald guy's feet in the doorway, twitching and jerking, with blood spraying out into the hall. We could hear growling and gurgling sounds, as well as the sound of ripping meat.

"I'm getting the fuck out of here," I said, squirming away from the bearded fat guy.

Then a door broke open and several people from the big orgy fell into the hallway. They all had black splotches on their faces, beady black eyes, and barbed wire teeth, just like the cat woman. When they saw us, they screamed in an inhuman bat-like pitch. Then they charged.

"Run!" the Punisher cried.

We took off down the hallway, but the Punisher didn't make it far until he ran out of breath and slowed down. I kept going, leaving him behind.

Down the hallway, a bouncer was being ripped apart by a rabid bug-eyed gray alien woman. Another bouncer was in the air, held up by a seven-foot-tall rabid deer woman, her antlers were impaled through his chest and stuck in the wall.

"What the fuck is going on?" somebody said as they ran behind me.

I turned to see it was Maria, the Mexican girl. She was running alongside me, following me out of there. She didn't recognize who I was.

"What are those things?" she said.

I didn't answer her. I didn't care what they were. After passing several torn apart Pinky bodies, we got to the stairwell and ran down to the main lobby.

The lobby was pure chaos. They were ripping each other apart down there. Tons of fuck-mutants had gone rabid and were attacking the other freaks. Because all of them were so oddly mutated, I couldn't tell which ones had the black splotches. I couldn't tell which ones were attacking and which ones were running away.

"Holy shit," Maria said, when she saw the chaos.

"We won't be able to get through them to the exit," I said. "We need to find another way out."

"That's the only way out I know of," she said.

One of the crazed fuck-mutants saw us and charged for the stairwell door. It was a red, horned man. He looked like a minotaur. I closed the door on him. Horns first, he charged into the door and nearly knocked me off my feet. I held the door shut. He slammed into it again. His horns pierced through the metal, nearly cutting into my hand. Maria had ditched me, she was running up the stairs. I let go of the door and followed after.

When I looked back, the minotaur man was trying to pull his horns out of the door, but all the act did was hold the door closed so the other rabid mutants couldn't get through. Upstairs, Pinkies were being ripped apart by the fuck-mutants. The hall was full of them. There was no way we'd be able to get by them all.

"Where do we go?" I asked.

"We should get to the Pinky Lounge," Maria said. "Follow me."

She led me through a dungeon room. Arms and legs were dangling from torture racks, but the only sign of the bodies they were once attached to was a trail of blood leading out into the hall. On the other side of the dungeon, we went through a door into a new hallway. This one was empty, outside of a lot of blood splatters on the walls and carpet. We ran around the corner and bumped into the Penetration Punisher.

"What do we do?" he cried.

"Pinky Lounge," Maria said.

We followed her through the labyrinth toward the Pink Lounge, but the doors were already shut. Two rabid fuck-mutants were banging on the outside of the doors, trying to get in. Before we could turn around to go somewhere else, five rabid freaks piled into the hall behind us. We were trapped on both sides.

When the fuck-mutants at the door noticed us, they turned around. I recognized one of them. It was the woman with four breasts and vampire fangs—which had now become barbed wire fangs. Her eyeball nipples were cold black balls. The other mutant had a lollipop for a head. They slobbered white foam as if they were salivating, then they charged us.

Maria and the Penetration Punisher just froze up. They didn't try to run or defend themselves, as if they had given up. I was just about to give up, myself. Without Lisa, my life was over. My boss would surely fire me for becoming a mutant. I would lose my income and my home. I'd be homeless and probably couldn't even prove my identity anymore. I wouldn't be able to get another job. I would probably end up prostituting my new body just to get by. That wasn't a life I wanted. I decided that I would be better off dead.

But something deep inside of me wanted to survive. It happened almost subconsciously. As the rabid fuck-mutants charged me, I felt long tentacle-like hands reaching out for them. It was my hair. My hair grew fifteen feet out of my head and attacked them. Two black locks wrapped them, around their throats, and picked them up off the ground. They struggled, trying to break free of the hair bondage.

Although it happened instinctually at first, I quickly found myself able to control my tentacle hair. I raised the mutants high over our heads to get them away from the door to the Pinky Lounge.

"Go," I told Maria and the fat guy. "I'll keep them back."

Maria ran to the doors. As she banged on them for help, the Punisher couldn't move. He just stared up at the creatures as I held them in the air.

My locks of hair tightened around their throats, strangling them. They thrashed around as their faces lost color. I tossed the lollipop-headed guy against the wall and his neck snapped. He fell to the ground, limp. Then I choked the life out of the four-breasted woman, her barbed wire teeth chomping in the air until she died.

I wasn't sure if there were any people inside of the Pinky Lounge, but if there were they weren't answering. Maria kept knocking, though, and begging for them to open.

"We're all right," she said. "We're not like them. Please let us in."

As the other five rabid fuck-mutants came at us, I grabbed three of them with more locks of my living hair. Then, with another lock, I pulled a giant monster dildo out of the ass of one of the infected mutants. As the last two ran at me, I clobbered them with the dildo, knocking one of them unconscious. Then I stabbed the other one with it. The dildo broke through his ribcage like a stake through his heart. He died instantly.

As the three mutants were dangling in the air, I smashed two of them together skull-first. Bits of brain crumbled onto the floor. Then I wrapped all of my locks of hair around the last mutant's arms and legs. He wiggled and squealed. His green turtle shell body wiggling helplessly in my hair-grasp. Then his body exploded into a bloody shower, as my locks pulled his limbs in opposite directions, quartering him.

When the Penetration Punisher saw the last of the mutants die, he said, "You're one tough sexy bitch."

I nodded at him. For some reason I did feel tough and sexy. I was beginning to like my new body. When Maria told the people inside the Pinky Lounge what I had done, and that all of the rabid fuck-mutants were dead, they finally opened the door and let us in.

There were nine people alive in the Pinky Lounge. About twenty corpses were also there. Most of them were Pinkies, but there were also a few super freaks.

"What are those things?" Maria asked the people in the lounge, as they reinforced the doors.

Somebody stepped forward. "It's an STD."

It was Cory. She was still alive. When she saw me, our Hello Kitty eyes locked. I was surprised she called it an STD and not an STM.

"Well, I've never heard of it before," Maria said.

"It might have never existed before tonight," Cory said. "New STDs pop up all the time. Sometimes they're created by combining two existing STDs. Perhaps somebody with Ultra Violence slept with somebody who had Brain Death or Ravenous Hunger."

The Penetration Punisher stepped forward. "Or maybe that's just what *they* want you to believe."

Everyone looked at him. They gathered around. He stood there with his little S&M outfit and hood, ready to explain his wild theory.

"Maybe the government created the disease," he said. "They hate these clubs and the freaks that are spawned from them. I bet they infected the water or something so that all the mutants would kill each other. It's a perfect way to get rid of us. They could just blame it on a new STD. It would also scare a lot of people away from coming to these places in the future."

Most people wrote him off as a conspiracy nut, but a couple people believed his story.

"It's bullshit," Cory said. "This kind of disease was bound to happen. With all the other varieties out there, I'm surprised this one hasn't happened already."

There was a banging on the door. Then multiple bangings. The rabid fuck-mutants were gathering outside the doors. When I looked around the room, I realized we were trapped. No windows. One door.

"What are we going to do?" asked a petite blonde girl. She was the same one who was looking for Breast Growth earlier.

"We wait here until help arrives," said the bartender in a shaky voice, holding a bloody broken vodka bottle like a dagger.

"That door isn't going to last long," Cory said. "We're going to have to run for it."

"Are you kidding?" said Maria. "Do you know how many infected people are down there? They outnumber us thirty-to-one."

"What about windows?" I asked. "I'm sure we could climb down."

"There aren't any windows in this place," said the bartender. "They bricked them all over. We're stuck here."

"We're going to have to fight them," said the Penetration Punisher.

They all thought he was nuts.

"How?" asked the petite blonde. "Those things have claws and razor teeth. They're monsters."

The fat guy pointed at me. "This bitch took out seven of them by herself."

They all looked at me.

"There's no way I could fight more than a few of them at once," I said. "As soon as I entered that lobby, I'd last two minutes, tops."

The group frowned and looked at their shoes. I thought about what they said for a moment.

"Unless... " I began. I had an idea. A horrible, horrible idea. But it was the only thing I could think of that could work. "What if we all had my STD?"

I looked at Cory and said. "I killed those creatures with the Hair Tentacles STD you gave me. If everyone here had it then we could probably fight off those demons."

"How did you kill them with Hair Tentacles?" Cory asked.

I gave her a demonstration. My hair grew out of my head and picked up three people gently by their waists. The Pinkies squealed as they were lifted into the air.

"Huh?" Cory said. "I've never done that before."

She tried it herself and was able to pick up the Penetration Punisher. Judging by the fat man's face, he seemed to find the act of being lifted by a beautiful woman's hair to be very arousing.

"Amazing," Cory said, as she bounced the Punisher up and down like a baby.

I told her, "You've been so focused on the visual appeal and sexual application of these STMs that you never noticed how useful they could be. Many STMs are practically super powers."

"So if we all have Hair Tentacles, we'll survive?" Maria asked.

"No, that's not good enough," I said. "We need more STMs than just Hair Tentacles."

I started collecting everyone's STD badges. "Give me all of your STMs. I want to see what we have here."

When I got them all in a pile, I scanned through each of them, looking for ones that could help us fight the maniacs outside.

"Antlers," I said, pointing at the guy with antlers growing all over his skin like jagged spikes. "Flexibility." I pointed at a rubbery-looking woman. "Iron fists." I pointed at a big guy in the corner. Then I listed more. "Long Jump, Razor Toes, Poison Tongue, Spike Tail." The list went on.

I dropped the badges. "We're going to combine them together. Each of us will get all of our STDs. Then we'll have these abilities collectively. We'll be a small army of powerful killing machines. We'll be able to fight our way out of here."

Everyone was quiet.

Then the short blonde girl said, "I don't want any freakish STDs."

Another guy agreed. The bartender did as well.

"It's the only way we can survive," I said. "Either you're with us or we leave you here."

Cory stepped forward. "I'm with him. We have to do whatever it takes if we want to get out alive. We die as humans or we survive as freaks."

It took them a few minutes, but everyone eventually agreed, no matter how much they bitched about it. The only way out was to become stronger mutants than the ones that wanted to kill us.

So then we had an orgy. I recommended exchanging blood, but that wasn't the way Cory wanted to handle it. She convinced the others that one last orgy before we went into battle was the way to go. The others agreed. They figured if they were going to fill their bodies with hideous STDs they might as well have fun doing it. Everyone got a chance to fuck each other. We each went from person to person, around and around, in a big pile.

At first, I took no pleasure in the sex I was having. Having sex as a woman was just too weird for me. If I had been bisexual, like Cory, it might have been different. But I couldn't help but feel as if I was being violated every time a penis went inside of me, especially when I was fucked by the Penetration Punisher whose beard was itchy against my breasts when he sucked on my nipples. I just tolerated it and prayed it would be over soon.

But after a while, I got into it. I stopped viewing my sex partners as a group of individuals. Instead, I saw them as one big entity. I wasn't having sex with a man or a woman, but a large blob of interconnected people. We were coming together, sharing our diseases, growing together into one.

By the time we were done, all of us were the same. We all had the same modifications. All of us had the same antlers growing on our arms, the same Hello Kitty Eyes,

CARLTON MELLICK III

the same striped skin, the same spiked tails, the same long waving tentacle hair. Those who were women were now men. Those who were men were now women. Other than that, we all looked the same. The only person I recognized after the change was the Penetration Punisher, who was now an obese woman with soggy breasts larger than her head.

We opened the doors and attacked the rabid mutants on the other side. We grabbed them with our tentacle hair and ripped them apart with our antler spikes. We cut down everything in our path. Mutant heads went flying through the hallways, bodies were torn in half.

When we found another group of survivors locked in one of the hot tub rooms, we had a second orgy. We obtained more powers and became even stranger mutants.

While I had sex with a tentacle-armed mutant, I heard news coming from my vagina. It sounded as if they were reporting this incident on the radio. I couldn't hear very well with a tentacle-penis in me, but I'm pretty sure what was happening at the Demon Seed was becoming world news.

Then we found another group of survivors who called for our help from the third floor. Their STDs melded with our STDs. Four more orgies later, we were more than powerful enough to go to the main lobby.

Two mutant armies collided once we got downstairs, but we had the upper hand. We were smarter and more clever with our combined STDs. The Penetration Punisher's Math Power helped us strategize our attacks. Cory's Tentacle Hair STD helped us throw mutants out of our way. Although they outnumbered us, we cut them all down without losing a single person.

When we got outside, we saw the streets were also full of rabid mutants. They must have spread their disease to more people out in the streets. We heard gun shots in the distance. The military had come in to clean up the mess. By morning, all of the rabid mutants were dead and,

78

although we were hideously deformed monstrosities, we had survived the night.

It's been thirty years since that night at the Demon Seed. It seems like another lifetime ago. I never saw Lisa ever again after that. I never saw my home or my job. Like illegal aliens, the lot of us were captured and taken away. Because of the Narcolepsy Maria had given all of us, we were vulnerable to capture as soon as we all passed out in the middle of a fight.

It was the military who made the call. They saw us battling the rabid mutants in the street, using our abilities to wipe them out and stop them from killing any more innocent Pinkies. The officers realized how dangerous we had become. We were labeled a threat to the safety of the American people. Partially out of fear, partially out of disgust, we were taken from our society and brought to a deserted island in the middle of the Pacific Ocean. We've built a new life for ourselves here, a new society with new customs and ideals. It's a primitive way of life, but we have adapted to it, embraced it.

We call ourselves New Humans, and see ourselves as a completely different species of people. I have a husband, who was once the Mexican girl Maria, and we had three kids together. I also had a child with Cory, who was conceived at the Demon Seed when I was last a male.

Our children were born with all of the same STMs we have. Because we live far away from the mainland, we never get any new STMs. Our children see our freakish appearance and abilities as normal. All they know about the world we left behind is what they hear from the voices that come out of their privates whenever they are sexually aroused. They've never seen regular humans before, but if they did I'm sure they would think that *they* were the weird-looking ones.

The only transformation our children ever go through is when they have sex for the first time. When they have sex and lose their virginities, their gender is changed. So the children who are raised as girls become men later in life. The boys become the women in adulthood. It has completely killed sexism in our society. There also isn't racism and as far as sexuality goes, almost everyone is considered bisexual, because nobody goes through life without having sex with members of both genders.

To you it might seem like an unusual way of life, but to us it is just life. We are lucky to have it. If you're ever in the southern Pacific seas I recommend you come pay us a visit. Our homes might not be as modern as the ones you're used to living in, but our orgies are second to none.

CITY
HOBGOBLINS

☺

There's more of them today, infesting the streets.

With their rotten grape skin, wooden horns, and hair-spray eyes.

"Don't play so loud," Lenny whispers at us from the door of the band room. "They're going to hear you."

We've got to practice for tonight's show, a gig over in the tower shops with some band called Slaughter Shoes. Only we're trying to keep quiet. Don't want to attract any of them, don't want them to know we're here, so we're playing without amps. I'm whispering my vocals and Ass Fort, our obese drummer, is smacking his legs with his sticks.

"We can't get any quieter," I tell him.

"Your guitars are still too loud," he says, aiming his pointy troll nose at me.

The guitar player, Stag, spits at him. "Get the fuck out."

"There's probably a dozen of them just outside," Lenny whisper-whines. "They can hear you. I swear they can hear you."

Stag scratches his nuts at Lenny.

I put my bass down. "We'll take a break until they leave."

"Yeah, fuck it," Ass Fort grunts, his shirt covered in sweat stains and mustard. "Let's drink some beer."

☺

Lenny, with his black hoody and old lady glasses, is sitting at the window watching the creatures wandering the streets, playing with his slidey skin. Even though he's always been skinny, Lenny's flesh is baggy like he's just lost half his weight. He can move his baby elephant tattoo from his wrist to his elbow by sliding his loose sleeve of skin back and forth. It wouldn't be so gross if he didn't fidget with it so much, like he's jerking off.

Stag always tells him he needs to get his arms circumcised.

I used to know Lenny back in high school, back when people called him a band fag. A drummer in the marching band who took art classes with me. We sat at the same table. My brain was usually pretty fuzzy from smoking groo at lunch.

As I tried my best to imitate H. R. Giger with embarrassing results, Lenny sat there quietly, staring at his blank sheet of paper. "What're ya going to draw?" I'd ask, but he would never respond. He was deep in concentration, like he was drawing a masterpiece within his head, and just needed to figure out a way to set it free. In the last ten minutes of class, he would begin to twitch. The twitching would brew in his baggy muscles, building up like a volcano ready to rupture. After six or seven minutes of twitching and sweating and the entire class watching/giggling with anticipation, he would then put his pencil to the paper and an explosion of lines would pour out. He would draw faster and faster, as if trying to purge the image out of his mind before it faded away. His back arched, his face two inches away from the page, nostrils flared, biting down on his lip, holding his breath for the most intense three minutes of artwork the world would ever see.

Only, nobody ever saw his work. His face would cover up most of what he was doing and his hands would hide the rest. And once the bell rang, Lenny would leap from his seat and crumple up his work into a tight little ball and bury it deep inside of his backpack, then charge out of the room, pushing people out of his way. The art teacher never got anything from him, didn't question him about it either.

The art teacher mostly just sat in the corner of the room staring at the chalkboard. Sometimes he'd crawl under his desk for a nap. Sometimes he'd shovel bagels between his flakey dry lips.

I guess that teacher's probably dead now.

The infestation is overwhelming on that side of town.

☺

Eventually Lenny and I became friends. Once he stopped playing Dungeons & Dragons and joined my punk band. I was hesitant at first. At the time, that band was my life. I didn't know if I wanted to bring such a creepy weirdo into my life, but drummers were in high demand. He worked out okay and turned out to be a nice guy. Our band was together for a few years, but we mostly just played parties and a couple empty bars.

After the band broke up, I started a new one with Stag and Ass Fort. Lenny joined some straight-edge-in-your-face-vegan-hardcore band, where he was happy. We stayed friends though. Even became roommates. Still are. But my other roommate, Stag, just hates the guy.

☺

"There's not that many," Stag says to Lenny, looking over his shoulder at the creatures outside. "You're such a douche."

Stag, which is short for Stagnant, calls the creatures *hobgoblins*.

There are many different species of hobgoblin. There are the crispy black demons, the octopus-limbed cat women, the white rubbery snail people. A new breed of them appears every day. They came out of a doorway called the *walm* in the center of the city. That's what they say. Lenny's been dying to go out there and check the walm out, but it's all the way across town and the streets are becoming too dangerous. If you run into the wrong type of hobgoblin you're going to be ripped to shreds.

Stag takes off his crusty shirt and sits in a chewed wicker chair. The tattoo of his face on his face is mostly shadowed by his Irish-green anarchy cap.

"Oi!" he says to Ass Fort in the kitchen.

Ass Fort nods and throws him a beer.

"Are we gonna get paid for this shitty gig?" Ass Fort asks.

"Yeah," I say. "A little. Probably not enough to cover your bar tab though."

"I don't think any amount of payment can cover my bar tab," he says.

☺

We sit in silence sipping our beers, staring at the television screen with a crack down the middle.

The television isn't on. It doesn't work. Ass Fort tried to use it as a chair a few months ago and his weight broke the insides. Still, we find our eyes glued to the screen. A natural habit maybe. Even when we speak to each other, we keep our eyes focused on the tube. Like we don't want to miss anything.

I pick up my sketch pad, wipe the groo residue off the cover, and begin to draw some sharks.

"You're thinking about her again, aren't you?" Stag asks me.

I shrug at him, curling one of my dreadlocks around my finger.

"You're not the only one who wants her back," he says.

I break my pencil lead at him.

"I was the one she loved," I say.

"She has no idea how to love," he says.

☺

Stag and Lenny have much more in common than they'd care to admit. For starters, they both played Dungeons & Dragons for years. They might have even played together in tournaments. My first guess was that Stag played as a fighter or a thief and that Lenny played as a wizard. But it was not that way at all. Lenny preferred to play as a thief and Stag played as a one-eyed gnome illusionist named Guko who had a white braided mustache growing out of his nostrils. He even DMed a campaign once.

You wouldn't think of Stag as the nerdy type these days. He's a big guy and mostly muscle. He punches the walls when he's angry. He breaks beer bottles over his head to impress the ladies. Yet, he has a Boba Fett poster on his wall and an Atari 2600 game system shaped like the starship Enterprise.

He's also writing a book about vampires in space. It's about 1,000 pages long and nowhere near completion. He won't let anyone read it. He'd rather burn it than let anyone read it.

☺

After a few beers we get back to practicing. There are still plenty of hobgoblins outside, perhaps a few more than before, but we have drowned our worries in alcohol.

"Too drunk to fear," Stag says.

He says *too drunk to fear* all the time. That's his motto. He has it tattooed on his ass.

Lenny isn't too drunk to fear. His twitchy body sits in the corner of the band room to monitor our volume. Whenever we get too loud, he gives us an angry thumbs-down until we soften our voices and guitar strokes. Then he'll give us an okay sign and go back to sliding his arm skin back and forth.

Our hit song is called "Glass Sandwiches."

We tend to practice that one every other song because Ass Fort likes it so much, he likes anything having to do with sandwiches, and screams *Glass Sandwiches!* after every song in a drunken fury even if we just finished playing Glass Sandwiches. Then he laughs and wheezes like he's completely baked and has no idea what he's doing, which is pretty much the truth. It is also our most requested song at shows, but I wouldn't say it's our best.

My favorite song is the one I wrote for *her*. I never told Stag the song was about her, but I'm sure he knows. It's kind of obvious. Sometimes I hate Stag for sleeping with her. Sometimes I hate him for not loving her like I do. But if it wasn't for him, I never would have been with her. I never would have fallen in love.

He says it's because it was my first time. You always love the one you give your virginity to.

☺

There's a crash in the living room.

"I told you!" Lenny cries.

We take our guitars with us as weapons.

Stag sticks out his tongue like Gene Simmons at Ass Fort and whispers "Too drunk to fear." Ass Fort raises his beer at him in cheers.

Outside the band room, there aren't any hobgoblins trying to get in. But the window is shattered all over the puke-stained couch. In the middle of the floor there is a small green ball with squirming tentacles.

"What is it?" I ask.

"It's alive and shit," Stag blurts.

"It's a baby," Lenny says. "A hobgoblin baby."

☺

Me: What are we going to do with it?

Stag: Toss it back out the window.

Lenny: No, you can't do that. It's just a baby.

Me: We don't know what it is. It's something from the walm. It could be poisonous or diseased.

Ass Fort: Let me step on it.

Lenny: Don't you fucking dare.

Ass Fort: Pussy.

Lenny: It's a living thing!

Ass Fort: Pussy.

Me: It's squiggling at Lenny.
Stag: It's got a woody for him.
Ass Fort: It wants your balls.
Lenny: It knows I want to help it.
Ass Fort: It knows you want to put it in your underwear.
Me: I'm telling you, the thing's not safe.
Lenny: I'm not just going to toss it back out there.
Stag: What are you going to do? Be its mommy? Keep it for a pet?
Lenny: If I have to.

☺

Lenny looks out of the window, searching for where the creature came from. There's nothing out there.

It's twilight. The streets are empty of hobgoblins. The city is most quiet at dawn and at dusk. The day creatures have all gone back to the sewer and there's still a couple hours before the nocturnal ones come out. Those tend to be the more dangerous hobgoblins. Luckily, we'll be at the club and off the streets by then.

"We better get the van loaded up," I say.

"I'll take the drums apart," Stag says.

Stag's always the one who takes the drums apart. Ass Fort might be the drummer, but he's usually too drunk to bother himself with the construction or deconstruction of a drum set. Actually, he's usually too drunk to bother himself with learning to play drums properly either. Luckily we're a punk band and don't give a fuck.

☺

Lenny wraps the baby hobgoblin in a towel, places it gently in a box, and brings it into his room.

I follow him.

His room looks more like storage than a bedroom. All of his possessions are in boxes stacked from floor to ceiling, boxes spilling out of his closet, boxes stacked on top of his dresser, boxes on his bed. He has no posters on the walls. No junk on the floor. It's like he just moved into this place yesterday, only he's lived here for a few years.

"You're not seriously going to keep that thing are you?" I ask.

"Of course," he says. "You know I'm pro-life."

"Lenny," I say, "how many times do I have to tell you pro-life is a stance on abortion."

"Yeah, well I'm pro-life when it comes to all issues. If there's anything in my power I can do to keep a living being alive I will do it. Even if it's something that came out of the walm. Even if it's dangerous."

"You weren't like this before you joined that vegan hardcore band."

"Pete," he squints his eyes at me, "shut the fuck up."

Then he pushes me out of the room and closes the door.

I stumble back into Ass Fort's giant belly and he laughs.

"He really is going to have sex with it, isn't he?" Ass Fort says. "I wonder if he'll let me watch... "

☺

Ass Fort isn't just a fat lazy half-assed drummer whose only passion in life is drinking beer. He also has a passion for fucking things. And by things, I mean *all* things. It doesn't matter what it is. It could be a dangerously obese woman, a crippled elderly man, a small mammal, a toaster, a corpse, a cheeseburger, a mail slot, a teddy bear, a cow brain. It doesn't really matter to him. If he can fuck it, he will.

We think it's pretty funny. He's this big fat hairy guy who's always drunk enough to fuck anything in sight. Sometimes I think he's that way just because he's trying to be funny. Like whenever we see a disturbingly deformed person hobbling down the sidewalk and laugh to ourselves, Ass Fort will step in and say, "I'm gonna go fuck it."

If Stag's motto is "Too drunk to fear" then Ass Fort's

motto is "I'm gonna go fuck it."

It's kind of funny now, but when he becomes an old man he's going to be the scariest pervert in the back of the porn shop.

☺

Ass Fort's main hobby these days, besides drinking beer and pretending he knows how to play drums, is looking for hobgoblins to fuck. He's always telling these wild stories about all these weird creatures he's been having sex with. From hog people to frog girls to anus-shaped plants.

Stag thought he was nuts, at first, until he saw some of the women Ass Fort was sleeping with. Not all of them were grotesque beasts. Some looked mostly human. They might have antennae or purple skin, but they were still attractive. So Stag started going out with Ass Fort on what they called their *missions*. Most of the hobgoblin girls were desperate. Living in sewers, on the streets. They were easily persuaded into sex if given some food or a place to sleep.

I didn't like it. Stag would bring these strange women home with him and they would hide out in his bedroom until he was tired of them and threw them out. I hated the way he took advantage of them, hated how dangerous it was, hated how jealous it made me to hear moaning through the walls.

Then he started experimenting. The women would get stranger and stranger. Less and less human.

☺

I drew the line when he brought home a shark woman. "Get her out of here!" I told him.

She was more fish than human. The rubbery flesh of a shark, the fins of a shark, the teeth and eyes of a shark. But amphibious, with human limbs, human-shaped face, human belly button, human breasts. It was the most dangerous hobgoblin I've seen. If it was desperate enough to sleep with Stag for food and shelter, it was probably desperate enough to murder us in our sleep... to use us as food and claim our home for shelter.

"No, she actually wants *me*," Stag told me. "She seduced me into bringing her back here. She doesn't care about the food or shelter."

That only worried me more.

"You've gone too far with this one," I said. "Take her somewhere else."

"Come on, it's cold out there."

"She leaves after you're through. I don't want her spending the night."

"Okay, fine."

"And she's the last. From now on, you get a hotel or take them back to Ass Fort's place."

"Whatever."

Then he disappeared into his room with her.

☺

I didn't sleep that night. I locked my door, pushed my desk in front of it. Waiting for Stag to run out of his room screaming, missing a limb or half his face. But nothing happened. The usual moaning came through the walls. Then quiet.

In the morning, the shark woman was still there, dipping her webbed fingers into a bowl of water and moistening her skin.

I took Stag aside, into the kitchen.

"What's she doing here?" I asked.

"Just hanging out," he replied.

"You agreed to get rid of her before morning."

"I tried," he said.

"And?"

"And she wouldn't leave."

"*Make* her leave."

"*You* make her leave," Stag said. "She scares the hell out of me. I'm not going to piss her off."

"She scares the hell out of you? *You* slept with her."

"Yeah, it was scary as hell."

☺

The day passed. She was still there. She slept with Stag again. He drank as much beer as he could and told me "Too drunk to fear" before crawling into bed with her.

She still wouldn't leave the next morning. She ate all of my cheerios and sandwich meat. Days passed and she became like a fourth roommate. Stag started to sleep out on the couch so that he wouldn't have to share a bed with her. We didn't know how to communicate but she seemed to act like she was one of us. She'd watch us practice, eat dinner with us, even drink with us.

☺

One night, she crept into my bedroom. Slithered under my sheets and made love to me. I didn't fight it. It was beautiful. Her rubbery skin sliding against me, nipples like pacifiers, her black ball eyes glistening in the darkness at me.

She tasted like spicy licorice. Not fishy as I imagined. She was sweet and filled with passion. I stroked the fin on the back of her head like it was hair, fell asleep in her tight strangling arms.

By the morning, I was in love. Stag said it was because I lost my virginity to her.

It's okay. I don't mind that I lost my virginity to a shark. I always told Stag that the only way I'd get a girlfriend would be if one jumped in my bed at night and started having sex with me. It's not that I'm an ugly guy, it's just that I can handle drenching my eyeballs in jalapeno juice better than I can handle rejection.

But things fell into place for me. I was in love and for

92

weeks she was like my girlfriend.

I didn't really understand who she was or where she came from, but I could feel her energy when we were pressed against each other. Her emotions seeped into me through the pores of her skin.

She wrapped herself around me while I wrote songs on my bass. She licked my neck with her white licorice tongue.

But I don't think she came from a monogamous culture. Though she slept with me, held me, loved me, she would sometimes slip into bed with Stag or Lenny after she was finished with me. I guess one man wasn't enough to satisfy her sexually. But I did know that I was the one she loved.

☺

Then one day she left. In the middle of the night, she just took off and never came back. I don't know why she left. Maybe she needed to get back to her own kind. Maybe she knew it just couldn't work out with us forever.

But I know for a fact that she didn't leave because she didn't love me anymore. The day before she left her love for me was probably the strongest it had ever been. Maybe that's what drove her away. She was frightened of her feelings.

I keep thinking that one day she'll come back. She'll crawl into my bed and squeeze her firm gray flesh against me until I cry.

But Stag says that will never happen. He says she got bored with us and is never coming back.

☺

The van is all packed up and ready to go.

"Who's going with who?" Stag asks.

"I'll drive the van," I say.

"Then you'll be driving solo."

"Why's that?"

"It's all packed up. Only room for a driver. I'll take Ass

93

Fort in my car. Lenny can drive his truck or come with me."

Ass Fort fills his Power Rangers backpack with cans of Pabst and heads out to Stag's car.

"I'll go with you, too," Lenny says.

"Well, we gotta leave now. I promised Gin I'd give him a ride so I gotta go all the way across the river to pick him up."

"A lot of hobgoblins over there," I say.

"There's a lot of hobgoblins everywhere," Stag says.

☺

They take off and I'm all alone in the house. It's getting dark. The nocturnal hobgoblins will be coming out soon.

I take a piss in the bathroom sink and look at myself in the mirror. I'm starting to get wrinkles. Only twenty-three, but I'm beginning to wrinkle. Must be from all the years of smoking and drug abuse. My body's going to hell. Just like this city. Ah, screw it.

If I had a motto like Stag and Ass Fort, mine would be: Ah, screw it.

I lift my shirt and examine the bumps on my chest. They have gotten bigger.

Stag warned me to use a condom when sleeping with the shark woman, but his warning came far too late. I didn't have a condom the first time she crawled into bed with me and couldn't stop the woman from putting me inside of her without protection.

Once these red bumps started appearing on my skin, Stag laughed his ass off.

"Serves you right," he said. "Now you've got some kind of weird hobgoblin STD."

The bumps are all over my torso like chicken pox. A couple dozen of them. They are very sensitive against my t-shirt, the fabric rubs them raw. I take some of Lenny's lotion out of his toiletry bag and rub it on the bumps.

They itch like hell when I put the lotion on them, but it's soothing once the skin absorbs it. I squeeze one of the bumps to stop the itchiness and a gray fluid squirts out.

"What the heck is that?" I ask my mirror image.

I wipe the fluid off my chest and smell it. It smells like her. Like black licorice.

☺

I change my pants and eat the last stick of string cheese, then cut my foot on the broken glass on the living room floor.

"Crap." It's one of the small slivers that you can hardly see but hurt like shit.

What the heck was that thing that came flying through the window anyway?

Some kind of blobby tentacled creature.

I can't believe Lenny wants to keep that thing. I should get rid of it while he's out of the house.

☺

Yeah, that's a great idea. He can't seriously take care of that creature. It's probably going to give us some alien virus or bite off Lenny's pointy nose.

Inside Lenny's room, the creature isn't in sight. He's packaged it away into one of his many boxes. Which one? They are all the same size and shape.

I open up his boxes one at a time. One contains neatly folded argyle socks. One contains He-Man cartoons on VHS. One contains a lunch box filled with Garbage Pail Kids trading cards and a chocolate brain.

And in one of them, there are hundreds of pieces of paper crumpled up into tight balls, piled up like a marble collection. I unfold one of them. It's a drawing. A drawing of a shark woman. *My* shark woman. It's very well drawn, the lines are jagged and scratchy but looks just like her... only she's masturbating with a high-heeled shoe. I open his other drawings and there are pictures of his vegan friends. They are naked and they too are masturbating with high-heeled shoes, in their rectums. Near the bottom there are drawings of his art classmates from high school, naked and masturbating with high-heeled shoes. I'm sure there's a picture of me in here somewhere, but I don't uncrumple any more of them.

☺

I find the creature in a box on the floor under his bed. He has put strips of newspaper down on the bottom of the box and has a measuring cup of water as well as a pickle jar lid filled with hamster food pellets. Why he has hamster food on hand, I have no idea. A puddle of gray ooze soaks through most of the newspaper and cardboard.

The creature's tentacles are squirming at me.

"You're getting dumped," I tell it.

When I pick up the box, the bottom flaps fall open and the creature drops out. Its tentacles wrap around my leg.

I shriek, topple backwards and shake my leg to get the creature off of me. It only tightens its grip.

I stand up and walk out of the room. The chitter of nocturnal hobgoblins outside the broken window. A needle pierces into me and I drop to the floor again. My mind is getting fuzzy. Poison. It's poisoned me. What the heck is this thing?

☺

I feel nice. The poison turns my brain into a cool summer morning. My hands feel like cotton candy and my belly is like a purring kitten. This is wonderful. I pull up my shirt and rub myself, caressing my STDs and inhaling the sweet licorice scent my love left behind.

This is the best high I've ever had. Better than groo. Better than slur corn. I've got to find more of these creatures. Bottle their poison and sell it at raves.

I think I'm in love.

☺

The alien cracks open. Its back pops into pieces and a gray ooze empties over my shin.

A dozen small people crawl out of the ooze. As small as my smallest finger, but human-shaped. They are fully mature, with breasts and pubic hair. Some of them have fins on their heads instead of hair.

Shark people babies. They are half human and half shark person. Some look mostly like sharks, others look very human, but most are a combination of the two. One of the male human-shaped babies stares up at me. It is a small version of me, looks exactly like me. My son.

These are *my* babies. The shark woman's babies. All our nights of unprotected sex has given us a litter. Buttery caramel feelings as the miniature people crawl up my skin, leaving trails of goo, to the STD bumps on my chest. They each take a bump into their mouths and suckle them like nipples.

One of them goes to my collar bone, my eyes focus on her. She looks human but with a large mohawk on her head like a fin. She drinks from a red bump. Gray ooze leaking down her neck and pooling at her bare breasts. She sees me watching her and stands up at me, wiping her mouth.

"Don't worry, Pete," the miniature woman says. "She does love you. I'm sure she will come back to you someday."

I nod at her and she goes back to suckling.

☺

A smile widens on my face. My eyes drift shut and I let my mind swim in thick gray fluids, wrapping my arms around my children to keep them warm.

Breathing in the spicy sweet scent of black licorice.

PORNO IN
AUGUST

They dropped us off by helicopter in the middle of the Atlantic Ocean, wearing speedos and sexy bathing suits, and now we are waiting for the director and crew to arrive. Staring at each other, wading in the ocean water miles and miles from any type of land.

"So what's this movie about?" asks the puffy blonde actress beside me, inside a child's floating tube with zebra patterns, trying to hold her hair away from the water.

Unlike any of the others, I am in a wetsuit with diving gear, even an oxygen tank. I have to take the mask and breathing tube from my face to respond. "Didn't you read the script?"

"I tried," says the woman, her breasts floating in the water under the tiny bikini top, "but it was too confusing to me."

"Well," I begin, "it's about... " My mind draws a blank. "We're in the middle of the ocean and... "

I don't remember.

I swear I read it just the other night, every line of it. I remember saying: "At last, a porn flick I'd be proud to act in. So new, so groundbreaking." But I don't remember a single word from it anymore. All I know is that it takes place in the middle of the ocean. I must be losing more brain cells than I thought.

I just stare at the blonde woman—Jenna, I think her name is—with a dumb/blank look. Then I turn and swim to another cast member, Randy, the only thing close to a friend in this business, probably because we both have a fascination with AMC automobiles, especially Matadors.

Randy is closing and opening his eyes, a zombie in the water, water wings on his arms to keep him afloat.

"Hey Randy, do you have a copy of the script?"

Salt water makes his eyes itchy and the sunblock on his nose doesn't seem to be helping. Turns to me, "No, I never got one. They said I'd get it last week. When I told them I never got one, they said one of the crew would give me a copy on the helicopter but the crew wasn't on the helicopter."

"They are coming by boat."

"Yeah, so I've never even seen the script. Did you forget yours?"

"I left it at home, we rarely follow the script anyway." I gaze down into the water to watch my flippers waving forth and back, inches below my flippers the deep blue water becomes darkness. "It's bugging me. I read the script, but I can't remember a thing about it. I remember really liking it, really-really liking it, but that's all."

Randy shrugs his beefy shoulders at me. "All I know is it's the biggest budget porn film this company has ever been willing to try." Chewing on a pruned finger, "And that it's shot entirely on location in the middle of the ocean."

Randy turns to the bald woman with a full suit of tattoos, who didn't bother to wear a bathing suit because she already has one tattooed on her privates. "Shady, do you have a copy of the script?"

The bald girl smiles at him, always smiling and twitching. "No, they wouldn't let anyone take it on the helicopter." She holds up her arm to scratch, tattooed up and down with sun-faces and dragon scales. "They didn't want them ruined in the water."

Randy calls to the entire cast of porn performers, "Does anyone know what this film is about? I was never given a script... "

Everyone looks at each other, frozen in question-faces, struggling with thoughts. I don't think a single one of them can give us an answer.

"I know what it's about," one of them says, deep voice.

Yes, it is King Soul, the big name of the film, the older

well-endowed black actor who's been doing these films for nearly twenty years. A real professional. Of course, he probably knows the script by heart, memorized it word for word, even the scenes he doesn't perform in. He's been known to treat porno scripts like he's acting in a real movie, or maybe even a play.

We all swim to him, circle around the King. He likes the attention. Big smile in his salty water goatbeard, scraggly like pubic hair.

"So what's it about?" I ask.

"Well, it's about a bunch of people stranded in the middle of the ocean. There's some sex. Parts of it are filmed on an island. Lots of other weird stuff too."

"Kinky stuff?" Shady asks, curling her fingers excitedly.

"Freaky stuff?" Jenna seems concerned.

"I mean... Well... " King Soul begins. "Well, just weird stuff. Unusual stuff. Like that stuff in art theaters."

"Like what?" I ask.

The King thinks about that for a minute, a hand in his crusty facial hair.

"Not sure," he says, and we groan in response. "I read it so long ago it might all be false memory. I had a couple dreams about the movie. Not sure what was the script and what was dream now."

"I can't believe how unorganized this is!" Randy squawks. "They said how important it was for us to actually read the script for once, but not a single one of us can remember a single detail!"

"Speaking of unorganized... " I say, softly. "Does anyone know when the crew is going to get here?"

Our eyes wander for the director's ship, looking to the horizons. Nothing. The ocean stretches for miles in all directions with no foreseeable end.

"How are they going to find us?" Jenna, like a little child though the oldest woman here. "They promised they wouldn't lose me. I'm scared of oceans."

"They can't lose us," King Soul says.

He holds up a small mechanism like a walky-talky with a blinking red light on it. "I was given this tracking device. They know exactly where to find us. They's just late, that's all."

You got to look up to Soul, everyone in the business does. He's so calm, has everything under control. They say he even graduated from college but doesn't ever brag about it. Half of us didn't even make it through high school. Hell, I only got a GED. But he's not the only one, we look up to Shady as well sometimes. She's been taking art classes at the community college for as long as I can remember.

We are able to relax for now, but my legs are getting tired from treading water. I have to let myself float sometimes to allow the muscles a rest. Good thing we all have strong lower bodies from doing so many of these films. We are all in great shape, even old Soul, for this kind of legwork.

The eleven of us hold tightly together, keeping each other warm as the wind begins to pick up.

We stop talking to each other when the sun goes down.

Water smacking against our bodies in the quiet, skin shriveled and numb, thirsty.

The water begins to get warm around us, hugging us, like a bed.

I open my eyes. I see half the sky is murder-black, but there's a deep blue line on the other horizon, the sun about to come up.

I move my legs and my mind jerks clear. I remember where I am. My lower half numb in the warm water, waving my bare feet back and forth in the dark salty ocean. I am no longer wearing the wetsuit or diving gear, but now am in a speedo that is not at all mine. Perhaps I traded costumes with someone.

I'm lying on my back, my upper half floating on something soft and comfortable. I turn to my left. No one is in that direction. I look to the right. No one. I look behind me, in front of me. I'm all alone.

I feel something rub against me under the water. Screech and leap, splashes in the ocean, looking for what had touched me. It was a hand, a human hand. Jenna. She is floating face down in the water, still in her floating tube. I had been on her corpse, sleeping on her this whole time. Perhaps I am the cause of her drowning. I don't remember at all. Shivers creep my back as I watch her body rocking in the dim lighting.

"Where is everyone?" I ask the water, but the water is busy whispering to itself.

I lift Jenna's face up. In a delayed burst, liquid burst-pours out of her mouth and nose and ears and eyes. I tremble at the sight, looking closer. Her eyes are wide open but the eyeballs are missing. And there is nothing inside of her beyond the eyeballs either, hollow. She is empty inside, just a shell filled with water. Her skin, on the inside and out, has been bleached white, her mouth hanging open, greasy tongue dripping out. Like a fish's mouth.

"What happened to you?" I ask her.

She looks blank. Not horrifying or morbidly disfigured, just blank. Empty and sad. I let her slip through the floating tube and slowly sink into the shadowy depths, her empty corpse refilling itself with water.

I take her place in the tube, a tight fit but I'll be able to last for a long time without having to tread water.

The strip of light in the horizon is not growing any bigger. The sun doesn't want to come up anymore.

Did everybody drown? Perhaps they killed themselves... It wouldn't have been difficult, just take a deep breath of water and then all black. Maybe they are with Jenna now.

But Jenna...

What happened to her? Her insides... just disappeared.

Perhaps she never had any insides. Perhaps—

A voice.

Somewhere in the distance. I can hear it slightly. From the darkness. I can't see that far. There's a fog in that direction.

I hear the voice again. A little more distant. It is real though. I'm sure. Definitely someone trying to find me. Perhaps the director and crew have finally arrived by boat. Or they might have sent a search party for us.

"Over here," I holler to the distance.

Those assholes. Fucking assholes. They came too late. I'm the only one left now. Yeah, I guess I should be happy I'm actually being rescued, but everyone else is dead.

"Over here, over here," I scream.

I get closer to the voice, it gets closer to me. But... there aren't any boat sounds. Just a voice.

I recognize who it is. Randy. He's still alive.

"Randy!" I call to him.

His distant voice grows a little louder and louder until we are able to understand each other. Though we are still unable to see each other in the fog.

"What happened?" Randy cries. "I don't remember anything. Did the helicopter crash?"

"What do you mean?" I ask.

"The last thing I remember is getting on a helicopter to film the new movie on some island. Then I woke up alone in the middle of the ocean. It scared the shit out of me. Where are you?"

"I'm over here."

His voice is so close to me, but the fog is getting thicker. I can't see anything.

"Keep talking," he says.

"Don't you remember yesterday at all?" I ask him, paddling furiously.

"Yeah, we went to the bar and bought an eight-ball."

"No, that was the day before yesterday."

"No, it was last night, remember?"

"You must be delirious," I tell him. "Yesterday we were

dropped off in the ocean. How could you forget? That was the whole catch to the film. It was going to be filmed in the middle of the ocean. We were waiting for the director's boat to get here, but they never showed up."

"What are you talking about?" Randy yells. I think I can make him out in the distance. "The film was going to be some stupid runofthemill porno on a deserted island. It was going to be a Gilligan's Island parody."

"No it wasn't, Soul said it was an avant-garde porn flick set in the middle of the ocean."

"What are you talking about? That's impossible. For one, Americans do not do avant-garde flicks. And two, how the heck are we supposed to fuck in the middle of the ocean?"

My mind becomes dizzy. Is he confused or am I the confused one? I don't think I can think straight. My head's in pain from dehydration.

"It doesn't matter what happened," I tell him. "We're both probably delirious. In either case, we're in a shit of trouble."

Still swimming to each other, but we have yet to meet.

"Have you seen anyone else?" he asks.

"I woke up next to Jenna," I tell him. "She's dead."

"Do you think anyone else survived?"

"I doubt it. I only remember you and Jenna having stuff to float on. The rest of them would have been treading water all this time. I don't think they made it."

"So you think they'll find us?"

"Not if this fog doesn't clear up, I can't even find you."

And then Randy came into view, lying on his back to keep afloat. His water wings stretched to his sides.

"There you are," I tell him, paddling my feet in his direction.

His eyes closed. I grab his leg and pull him to me, just watching him in his relaxed position.

But he doesn't end this relaxed posture.

"Randy... " I reach my hand to his shoulder. "Come

on, stop fucking around."

And I jerk him to wake.

A popping noise. Randy opens his eyes and water boils out of the sockets, flowing out of his mouth and nostrils. I splash backwards, almost out of the floating tube, fumbling my limbs. Face dunks into the hot ocean. Try to reclaim myself, huffing/choking breaths.

A few minutes of calm-breathing and I slip the water wings from Randy, let him sink out of view.

"You too, Randy," I say to his silhouette beneath me. "You were empty inside just like Jenna."

They must not have had souls. Just hollow sad creatures without anything on the inside. I guess most people in the adult film business are without soul. Eventually, as I believe Jenna once told me, the business squeezes it out of you like juice, and then you don't really care about anything anymore.

A gush of water goes into my lungs and I cough myself into consciousness.

"Hey, look who's awake," Shady says, splashing water at me. And my eyes go in and out to see her face, her bald head shining in the dim light.

"Told you he'd wake up eventually," I hear King Soul from beside me.

I clear my head and look around. There are five of them with me.

"What happened?" I ask them. "The last thing I remember is finding Randy dead."

"That's all you remember?" Shady asks. "You didn't go unconscious until two days after we found you. And you told us you found Randy empty that morning."

"I don't remember seeing any of you since the first day. How long have we been out here?"

"How long, Grim?" Shady asks the skinny bearded biker

guy to my left.

"Eleven days," he says in a feminine voice.

Wait a minute.

"Eleven days?"

Shouldn't we be dead by now?

"The jellyfish have been keeping us alive," Shady says.

My questioning face wrinkles into more questions.

"You're the one who found them," Grim tells me, his face very bisexual in its features.

"Look," Shady says, jerking her dragon hand into the water and pulling out a transparent jellyfish as big as a head, squirreling at her wrist. "The first night we were out here you reached into the water and pulled one out."

"There's enough juices and nutrients to sustain us," Soul tells me, "But now we're starting to think they're poisonous, making us lose our memory."

"Here, we haven't fed you in awhile," Shady gives the curling jellyfish to me. "Eat this."

Biting into the live creature, twisting limbs around my face. Water. Cold fresh water gushes down my throat, and the creature stops moving.

"It's fresh water," I say.

"Yeah," Shady tells me. "Like a living water balloon."

A rubbery exterior with only water inside.

"There's hundreds of them all around us," some girl says. "But you can't see them 'cause they're clear."

After I chew its stretchy meat down, I gaze into the water looking for them. But there is nothing. Just crystal water.

"What happened to the others?" I ask.

King Soul: "Well, you said Jenna and Randy drowned. Toby and Camesis disappeared the first night like you. And Norma... Well, there's been... a shark that's been after us for the past few days. It picked off the weakest of us yesterday. You probably would've been next."

"What about the tracking device?" I ask.

"What tracking device?" Shady blinks her tattooed eyes.

"Soul has a tracking device," I tell them.

They have confused looks.

King Soul digs into his bag around his shoulder.

"Everything they gave me is in here," Soul says. "But I don't remember a... "

He's so shocked to see the device in his hand that he nearly drops it.

"That's it," I say. "But it was blinking before."

Soul clicks a button and the red light starts blinking again. "It was turned off... "

"We're saved," one of the girls says. "They'll find us now!"

Shady: "Thank God you remembered."

A wave of relief blows through them, but I am amazed they had forgotten about it. It's something I would never let leave my mind.

"By the way, wasn't there twelve of us supposed to be in the movie?" a girl asks us. She's the girl who was supposed to work with Shady in the lesbian underwater scenes.

"What do you mean?" Shady asks.

"They always have twelve cast members in every film they make."

"I don't know what you're talking about."

"No, that's right," Soul says. "They were always strict about that. But wasn't there twelve of us dropped off in the ocean?"

"No there were eleven of us," the girl says.

"Vixen," Shady puts her hand on the girl. "I think you're right. Hold on... There are the six of us, Norma, Randy and Jenna, Toby and Camesis. That's eleven."

"Who was the twelfth?" Vixen asks.

Shady: "You and I were going to fuck, Randy and Mark were going to fuck Jenna, Soul was going to fuck Norma and Camesis, Grim was going to fuck Toby. Who's left?"

The shy girl behind me, a newbie in the business, "I don't know who I am screwing?"

We all turn to her, Cyl I think her name is. Yeah, pretty sure it's Cyl.

A moment of clarity and my hand reaches up in the air.

"The little guy!" I scream.

"Who?" they ask.

"You know, the little man."

Soul: "Oh yeah, the midget."

"I'm screwing a midget!" Cyl screams.

"Not a midget," I say. "A little person. Remember, he always gets mad when you call him a midget."

"What's it matter?" says Soul. "Midget is just another word for little."

Vixen: "But what happened to him?"

"He was never on the helicopter," Grim says.

"Yeah, he was," Soul says. "The entire helicopter ride seems like a dream now, but I swear he was on it."

"Did he ever get off?" I ask.

"Yeah," Soul says, "he was swimming with us, making us laugh with his tricks."

Me: "Where is he then?"

Soul: "He must have disappeared like the others."

"Are you sure you didn't dream him?" Vixen asks.

"No," he says. "Of course not, I always confuse my dreams with memories."

"I'm glad he's dead," Cyl says. "I don't want to fuck a midget."

"Who was I supposed to sleep with?" I ask them.

"I already told you," Shady says. "You and Randy were going to do Jenna."

"No," I tell her. "You said *Mark* and Randy were."

They gaze at me.

"You *are* Mark," they say.

"No, I'm not... "

Wait a minute. What is my name?

"It's not Mark, it's... " I shake my head.

"Mark," Shady puts a dragon arm around me, "this is hard for us all."

"My name isn't Mark!" I shove her away.

"Then what should we call you?" Shady asks.

"Don't call me anything," I say, swimming away from her.

I wake one morning in the wetsuit again, praying I am not lying on another dead/empty body.

My eyes searching. I see King Soul sleeping, Grim holding him up. Cyl sleeping, with Vixen holding her.

And I turn my head, noticing Shady is behind me, making sure I don't drown in my sleep.

"You didn't sleep long," she tells me.

"I feel like I've been asleep for days," I tell her, rubbing my red eyes with salty numb fingers.

"You've been awake for days," she tells me, "and only slept for an hour."

"How long have we been out here?"

"You've forgotten again?"

I nod.

"We stopped counting a long time ago. A month or two, maybe."

My eyes burn spicy at her words, wanting to cry.

Shady says, "Our memories keep going in and out, especially after we sleep. We don't know how truthful our memories are anymore."

"I don't remember very much at all."

"Nothing's been worth remembering. We just take turns sleeping and eating jellyfish all day. And sometimes one of us loses most of our memory and we have to explain a lot of things."

"What about the tracking device?" I ask.

"There is no tracking device," Shady says in a bent voice.

"What happened to it? Did it break? Sink?"

"No," Shady says. "Soul opened it. There was nothing inside. Just a box with a blinking red light."

"Are you sure?" I ask.

"It was just a prop for the film," she says. "Not a real tracking device."

"Well, what about the shark?" I ask.

Shady pauses.

"What shark?"

"There was a shark, they said it killed Norma."

"No," Shady says. "Norma drowned. There's been nothing but jellyfish out here."

"No, they said it was a big shark that killed her in one bite."

"Your memory is playing tricks."

A high-pitched scream and everybody jerks upright. A fin is in the water, violently splashing next to Cyl. Vixen pulling the young girl away from the splashing fin.

"A shark," Grim screams and everyone swims together in a tight ball.

The shark fin lowers into the water. Cyl shrieking at the top of her lungs. We hold her from thrashing, arms whipping at us.

"My feet," she screams. "Watch my feet."

We pull her into the floating tube, exposing the shark bite to us.

We jump away from her when we see it. Her feet are missing. But there is no blood. Her legs are hollow, nothing inside at all. Water gushes out of the holes and into the ocean.

When she sees her legs, Cyl stops screaming. Like she was never really in pain. Her eyes drop wide. Just staring at the stream of water draining out of her hollow limbs.

"What the hell are you?" Vixen screams.

The shark is circling in the background, but all of our attentions are on Cyl now.

Cyl is confused, shocked maybe, not saying a word, not breathing. She lifts her wrist to her eyes and examines it closely. Then she pokes a hole with a fingernail. A thin line of water sprays out like a cut vein. Everyone watching her, the shark behind us, as she begins to drink from her arm. Then she looks up and smiles.

"I'm like the jellyfish," she tells us.

And then she falls back, exhausted.

"I'm hot," she says. "I'm so hot. The water... "

Shady swims to her, staring into her hollow legs.

"She's right," Shady says. "She's like a jellyfish."

They all sigh, like the whole mystery has been solved.

Then Shady bites into her arm, ripping the rubbery skin from her. Cyl doesn't scream, watching Shady chew her like a jellyfish. The rest of them join her, gnawing on Cyl's skin, water squirting out into their mouths.

I swim behind her as Shady chews the back of her head away. She's totally hollow inside. And I can see the back of her face.

"Stop doing that," Cyl says, and seeing her mouth move from the inside sends nails into my cricky neck. No vocal chords, no brain, no blood. How can she function?

"She's a jellyfish, Mark," Shady says, stuffing one of Cyl's empty breasts into my mouth. "Eat her."

"Wake up!" somebody screams through a megaphone.

I open my eyes to a small speedboat in front of me. A camera is pointed in my direction.

My vision clears and I see three men standing in the boat. A camera man, a sound man, and the director with his megaphone.

"We have a porno to make," he says. "No more sleeping on the job."

I don't recognize the man. He is not the director I remember. Actually, I don't remember any of these men. We've had the same director for years, we go drinking together, baseball games together, but these people are utter strangers, yelling at me like a drill sergeant. I'm not sure what the original crew looks like or what their names were, but these people are not them I'm sure of it.

"Start fucking," the director yells at me.

I see King Soul and Grim are double-teaming Vixen over there, lying on floating tubes, struggling to get a decent position.

112

I turn around to Shady, who was cradling me in my sleep. "When did they get here?" I ask her.

"A couple days ago," she whispers. "They've been working us day and night. I don't think we can do it anymore. They won't let us in the boat until they have enough decent footage for the movie."

"Go under water," the director screams, pointing his finger like God.

Shady and I are sucked under the water, jellyfish pulling us down, curling around our limbs and sucking us under the water. Invisible creatures forcing us together, my wetsuit rubbing against her tattooed flesh. We use my oxygen tank to take turns breathing as they pull us into the darkness. They open up a pocket in the crotch of my wetsuit, they slide up the insides of her legs, and then they shift us together like puzzle pieces.

I watch Shady through the mask, her eyes closed tight with fear and maybe pleasure, the jellyfish caressing the backs of our thighs and shoulders. But my mind jerks awake as I realize I feel nothing inside her. She is hollow/empty in there. I'm just moving in open space. I go soft. I cannot continue.

Over Shady's shoulders, the shark is returning, plunging at us for an attack. I grab her, force our way through the slippery jellyfish, her hollow body light enough to carry. We explode through the surface and Shady takes a gasping breath.

"Get back down there," the director screams at us.

"Shark! Shark!" Shady yells at him.

And the shark leaps out of the water, flying over our heads like its fins are wings. We all tweak our eyes when we see the shark has pink-peach skin and large human-like breasts underneath it. And it lands on the unsuspecting Grim, who had been hard at work between Vixen's legs until it came crashing on top of him. The shark begins squirming on top of him. It is screwing him. He screams at us for help, but we cannot move. He tries to scream again but the shark bites into his face, tears off his mouth.

Water gushes out of Grim's face, his head is hollow inside. His lower face missing, Grim's eyes look around, watching the shark/woman as she rapes him.

"Keep going! This is great!" the director screams, cheering for the shark. "This is what we've been waiting for!"

Vixen is pinned under Grim. King Soul slowly swims away without considering to help. Vixen pushing on Grim but they are hooked together by the floating tube and the weight of the shark.

Jerking arms, punches, but the shark will not stop fucking Grim and begins to eat more of his meat, ripping his arms from the sockets and slurping them down, devouring the rest of his head, chewing on his chest as she rubs her shark-breasts all over him.

"Oh, what a picture!" screams the director.

Vixen kicks the shark, trying to get away, and the shark snaps at her, taking her entire face off, and the shark continues its rampage on Grim's lower half. Faceless Vixen swimming blindly away.

"Mark," the director screams, "go fuck the shark in the ass!"

"My name isn't Mark," I respond, swimming away from the rapist fish.

At a safe distance, I turn to see Shady and King Soul sneaking onto the speedboat. The director shouts at me to return to have sex with the shark.

Soul, in his leopard speedo, has a sharp object in his hand. A knife maybe, or a broken beer bottle, something that he found close to him on the boat. And as the sound man turns to him, Soul slashes him in half, his whole body cut into two, folding backwards, empty inside. Water splashes at Soul, blinding him as the director and camera man turn to attack.

Vixen's faceless body is swimming in my direction, following my splashes. I try ignoring her, the horrifying look of a woman alive and swimming without the front half of her head.

I watch Shady out of the water. Her tattoos are like fish scales covering her skin, fighting the director with the boom stand, in her nudity, but with her illustrations she never really looks naked. She's a beautiful woman, even though a porn actress. But she's empty inside now, all of her beauty is only on the outside.

She punches the rod right through the director's chest, but the director continues swinging the megaphone at her. King Soul cuts the camera man's leg off, water emptying into the boat.

Vixen, the faceless creature, is behind me now. She grabs me and holds me, caressing my flesh.

The shark leaps into the boat, tearing into the camera man, and Soul is ripped in half longways.

His water empties out of him, but one half of him is still standing. One leg and one arm, balancing.

The sounds of the shark eating rubbery meat. Soul's left half stays upright just long enough to cut the director's head off, leaning to one side and popping his head right off of its neck, both of them crashing into the water.

Shady standing alone in the boat: Her face has a confused look as if waking into the situation without any memory of it ever happening. She jerks when she notices the shark in the boat, fucking and eating a man. And then she shrieks when she sees Soul's right half lying in the boat, wiggling at her. One by one, she tosses the men into the water, and the shark chases after them.

I try screaming at Shady, but she doesn't seem to hear me. She must be horribly confused. And Vixen holds me tight in place, won't let me swim to her, wrapping her legs around me.

Shady turns on the boat and speeds into the distance, the shark following close behind.

And I am alone in the ocean again. Alone with Vixen, the faceless abomination.

She is still caressing my body. I look into the back of her head because she has no eyes to look into. She moves me forward, hand around my skull to pull me closer to kiss her. But without a mouth, my face slides into her empty head and kisses the insides. The back wall of her head is slick and salty. I close my eyes, holding her tightly in the water.

I wake on a beach, staring up at a bright sun. Salt-foamy water simmering around me.

I sit up.

My clothes are a white tuxedo. My mind feels just as white, like a blank piece of paper.

The island is lush with vegetation and hills, a stream of water leaking from my nose. Walking up the beach, the sun following me like a camera. Like I am a television show to the sun. After a ways, I find a table with two seats. A white cloth covering it, with a centerpiece of wildflowers.

I sit down in one of the chairs, brushing the sand off of my tuxedo and hands. My face goes into the tablecloth, eyes drifting.

"Can I get you something, monsieur?" a scratchy voice asks me.

I lift my head and see a little man of three and a half feet standing on a log and wearing a white tuxedo almost identical to mine. He also wears a matching eye patch.

"Excuse me?" my mind spinning.

"Can I take your order, monsieur?"

I look at my hands as if a menu and then look back at the little man, my mouth agape, squinting my eyes.

"Yeah," I tell him. "Give me the roast beef."

"Very good, monsieur," says the little man, writing it down in a notebook . "What would you like as beverage?"

"Just water," I tell him.

"Very good, monsieur," he says, scribbling words in his notebook. "Are you meeting someone, monsieur? Or dining alone?"

"I don't know," I tell him.

There is a woman in my view striding along the beach. She sees me and waves, smiling wide. I do not recognize her but she seems to recognize me. The woman is nude but has a white dress tattooed to her body. Her head is bald of hair but has a white dinner hat tattoo, tilted to one side.

The smile grows even bigger once she sits at the little table across from me, saying, "Hello, Charles, isn't it a wonderful day today?"

"Yes," I say, half-smiling back to her. "One of the best I've seen."

Her vision lowers to my hand and her smile turns angry, shocked. "Oh my God! Your ring is crooked!"

She rips my hand from its resting place and adjusts a wedding ring that has been on my finger. Then she holds our hands together and I see she has a similar ring tattooed on her finger.

Once she decides my ring is lined up perfectly with hers, she pops her face up into my sight and brings back her very large smile.

"Your water, monsieur," the little man says as he taps a sandy glass on the table.

And the little man closes his one good eye and places his thumb in his mouth, biting it off at the tip. Then he fills my glass with the water from inside him.

I sigh as I take a drink, my hand still prisoner to the woman's grasp, trying to pull it away.

The small man scurries to her, "And for madame?" as I gaze into the distance to find another happy couple on the beach. A woman missing the front of her head, burying half of a black man in the beach soil, and the tide flows in without the consent of the moon.

AUTHOR'S NOTES

CANDY-COATED

I don't know why, but one thing I find absolutely hilarious is watching a buff dude trying to pick up chicks. It's even funnier when that buff dude thinks he's the awesomest human being on the face of the planet, even though everyone around him thinks he's the complete opposite. When I came up with the idea for this story, I thought: what if the buff dude had a lollipop for a head? And the story went from there. Truckers and cheese-tasting was the logical next step.

This was originally published in the all-fiction issue of *Vice Magazine*. They wanted me to send them something goofy, weird, short, and stupid, and I said, "Hey, I've got the perfect story for you!" It's actually one of my favorite short stories that I've ever written, and it will be appearing in the anthology, "The Best Bizarro Fiction of the Decade" later this year. I hope to write more like it.

Vice also did an audio recording of the story. The voice actress they got was Madelyn Burgess, whose voice you might recognize if you ever shop at Whole Foods. She does the voice that comes over the PA, telling you which register to use. That voice isn't just a pleasant female robot voice. It's a real person. And she did the audio version of the story, which you can listen to at the Vice Magazine website.

EAR CAT

So a large percent of the population is crazy about cats. But you know what those people are not crazy about? Gross cats. Once a cat gets old and slimy nobody wants to go near the thing anymore. I mean, I've seen a cat thats fur was infested with earwigs before. How the hell does a cat become infested with earwigs anyway? I'm not going to pet an earwig cat. Fuck that thing. I can pet myself a brand spanking new earwig-free cat any time I want.

This story is about a woman who finds herself trapped in a house with a gross cat. But this one is even grosser than an earwig cat. Instead of fur, it has human ears growing all over its body. If an ear cat actually did exist it would be pretty screwed. Nobody could love that thing. It would leak earwax all over your stuff, and it would always be listening to you. I hate when cats are always listening to me. They need to mind their own fucking business. Better yet, they need to get off their asses and do something useful for a change. Being cute just isn't going to cut it anymore.

FANTASTIC ORGY

Let's face it: sexually transmitted diseases need to be more awesome. I'm sick of all the blistery, itchy, puss-oozing sexually transmitted diseases out there. I want them to be more stylish, like STDs that give you cool Japanese surfer hairdos. Or STDs that make your skin blue. Or STDs that cause you to know all the lyrics to every REO Speedwagon song. Stuff like that.

Sexually transmitted super powers would also be nice. It would be pretty sweet to wake up one morning with adamantium claws after going to bed with Wolverine the night before. Then STDs wouldn't be something to shun. They would be more like trading cards. You give me your Vulcan Eyebrows STD and I'll give you my Glen Danzig Muscles STD. I guess you can't really call Vulcan Eyebrows STDs, since they aren't really diseases. They would be more like STEs (sexually transmitted eyebrows). But, whatever, let's forget about the technicalities.

I wrote Fantastic Orgy with this concept in mind. It

was probably the story I had the best time writing of the bunch in this book. I wrote it at the Sylvia Beach Hotel in the Harry Potter room, which was designed like a bedroom at Hogwarts. It's kind of disturbing to think that this story was probably somewhat inspired by Harry Potter. Harry doesn't seem like the orgy type.

CITY HOBGOBLINS

There's one thing that I think is missing from a lot of literature these days. Want to know what it is?

Two words: shark sex.

You know, there's a lot of furries out there who get so turned on at the sight of frolicking fox boys or slutty unicorn girls or stupid fucking dragon hermaphrodites. But if you ask me, there are way hotter anthropomorphic creatures out there: shark chicks. Yeah, maybe having sex with shark women isn't perfect. They urinate through their skin all over you and almost always try to bite your face off when they cum. But, you know, maybe I'm into that kind of thing. It beats butt-fucking a transvestite bunny-panda.

When bizarro author/publisher Cameron Pierce edited this collection, he said: "It's good, but there's so much shark sex..."

And, after thinking about it, I realized that there actually is quite a bit of shark sex in this book. I mean, in "Porno in August" some of the characters get raped by a shark with boobs. So, in order not to appear stupid, I said, "Well, yeah, of course there's a lot of shark sex in it. Shark sex is awesome!" And ever since then I've had to pretend that I think shark sex is awesome. But, you know... to be honest, I can go either way with shark sex.

This story was meant to be a prequel to my novels *Satan Burger* and *Punk Land*. It is set in the world of Satan Burger, featuring a few minor characters from the book. But it was mostly designed to be an origin story for the character Shark Girl from Punk Land. This story is about her shark chick mother and punk human father. It's kind of a love story. But, yeah, there's shark sex in it. This story was also inspired by the song of the same name by the British bizarro punk band *The Fall*, which is a band I've loved for a long time. It was originally published in "Perverted by Language: Stories Inspired by the Music of The Fall." I don't think the members of the band cared for the story very much. I don't think they liked any of the stories in the book. But, you know what? The anthology paid me. A lot. In advance. So suck on that, bitches!

PORNO IN AUGUST

This is probably my most successful short story, since it was published in *The Year's Best Fantasy and Horror*. It's also the earliest in this collection, written before I had a single book published. I consider this the first "real" short story I wrote. All stories that came before this I consider my "sell out" stories, because they were all stories that I didn't write for myself. I wrote them because I thought they were what the editors of sci-fi magazines were looking for. It's funny that the first story I wrote for myself was the one that editors were actually interested in.

Basically, I started with an absurd idea: a group of porn actors find themselves floating in the middle of the ocean with no real clue how they got there. Then I let the story unfold from there.

Every once in a while I'll get an email from a college student who is studying this story in their science-fiction literature class. They'll ask me what the meaning is behind the story. They'll say, "It's about the emptiness of the porn industry, right? That's why the porn stars become hollow inside?" And I'll say, "Uh, yeah, sure, sounds good." And they'll say, "And in the ending, when the midget bites his fingers off, that represents the brutal effect that pornography has on our society, right?" And I'll say, "Um, huh?" Then they'll say, "And the shark with boobs that jumps in the boat and starts raping everyone, that represents the oppressive nature of the porn industry and how pornography is actually raping our society's concept of sex when sex should be viewed as a beautiful experience shared by two consenting adults, right?" And I'll say, "What the fuck are you talking about? It's just a stupid story. Don't take it so seriously."

So just to be clear, this story is not an attack on the porn industry. Although if I were to attack the porn industry it would be to complain about how terrible it all is. Who the heck do they think is the target audience for porn anyway? Old men? I'm pretty sure only old men would find that stuff sexy. It's all the same boring crap over and over again. They say there's porn for everything on the internet. Bullshit. I've looked. It's all crap. If I were a porn filmmaker I'd put a little art into it. I'd film pornos in unusual locations, like in the middle of the ocean. Then I'd try to find a shark with boobs...

ABOUT THE AUTHOR

Carlton Mellick III is one of the leading authors of the bizarro fiction subgenre. Since 2001, his books have drawn an international cult following despite the fact that they have been shunned by most libraries and chain bookstores.

He won the Wonderland Book Award for his novel, *Warrior Wolf Women of the Wasteland*, in 2009. His short fiction has appeared in *Vice Magazine, The Year's Best Fantasy and Horror #16, The Magazine of Bizarro Fiction,* and *Zombies: Encounters with the Hungry Dead,* among others. He is also a graduate of Clarion West, where he studied under the likes of Chuck Palahniuk, Connie Willis, and Cory Doctorow.

He lives in Portland, OR, the bizarro fiction mecca.

Visit him online at **www.carltonmellick.com**

Bizarro books

CATALOG SPRING 2011

Bizarro Books publishes under the following imprints:

www.rawdogscreamingpress.com

www.eraserheadpress.com

www.afterbirthbooks.com

www.swallowdownpress.com

For all your Bizarro needs visit:

WWW.BIZARROCENTRAL.COM

Introduce yourselves to the bizarro fiction genre and all of its authors with the Bizarro Starter Kit series. Each volume features short novels and short stories by ten of the leading bizarro authors, designed to give you a perfect sampling of the genre for only $10.

BB-0X1
"The Bizarro Starter Kit" (Orange)

Featuring D. Harlan Wilson, Carlton Mellick III, Jeremy Robert Johnson, Kevin L Donihe, Gina Ranalli, Andre Duza, Vincent W. Sakowski, Steve Beard, John Edward Lawson, and Bruce Taylor. **236 pages $10**

BB-0X2
"The Bizarro Starter Kit" (Blue)

Featuring Ray Fracalossy, Jeremy C. Shipp, Jordan Krall, Mykle Hansen, Andersen Prunty, Eckhard Gerdes, Bradley Sands, Steve Aylett, Christian TeBordo, and Tony Rauch. **244 pages $10**

BB-0X2
"The Bizarro Starter Kit" (Purple)

Featuring Russell Edson, Athena Villaverde, David Agranoff, Matthew Revert, Andrew Goldfarb, Jeff Burk, Garrett Cook, Kris Saknussemm, Cody Goodfellow, and Cameron Pierce **264 pages $10**

BB-001 **"The Kafka Effekt" D. Harlan Wilson** - A collection of forty-four irreal short stories loosely written in the vein of Franz Kafka, with more than a pinch of William S. Burroughs sprinkled on top. **211 pages $14**

BB-002 **"Satan Burger" Carlton Mellick III** - The cult novel that put Carlton Mellick III on the map ... Six punks get jobs at a fast food restaurant owned by the devil in a city violently overpopulated by surreal alien cultures. **236 pages $14**

BB-003 **"Some Things Are Better Left Unplugged" Vincent Sakwoski** - Join The Man and his Nemesis, the obese tabby, for a nightmare roller coaster ride into this postmodern fantasy. **152 pages $10**

BB-004 **"Shall We Gather At the Garden?" Kevin L Donihe** - Donihe's Debut novel. Midgets take over the world, The Church of Lionel Richie vs. The Church of the Byrds, plant porn and more! **244 pages $14**

BB-005 **"Razor Wire Pubic Hair" Carlton Mellick III** - A genderless humandildo is purchased by a razor dominatrix and brought into her nightmarish world of bizarre sex and mutilation. **176 pages $11**

BB-006 **"Stranger on the Loose" D. Harlan Wilson** - The fiction of Wilson's 2nd collection is planted in the soil of normalcy, but what grows out of that soil is a dark, witty, otherworldly jungle... **228 pages $14**

BB-007 **"The Baby Jesus Butt Plug" Carlton Mellick III** - Using clones of the Baby Jesus for anal sex will be the hip sex fetish of the future. **92 pages $10**

BB-008 **"Fishyfleshed" Carlton Mellick III** - The world of the past is an illogical flatland lacking in dimension and color, a sick-scape of crispy squid people wandering the desert for no apparent reason. **260 pages $14**

BB-009 "Dead Bitch Army" Andre Duza - Step into a world filled with racist teenagers, cannibals, 100 warped Uncle Sams, automobiles with razor-sharp teeth, living graffiti, and a pissed-off zombie bitch out for revenge. **344 pages $16**

BB-010 "The Menstruating Mall" Carlton Mellick III - "The Breakfast Club meets Chopping Mall as directed by David Lynch." - Brian Keene **212 pages $12**

BB-011 "Angel Dust Apocalypse" Jeremy Robert Johnson - Meth-heads, man-made monsters, and murderous Neo-Nazis. "Seriously amazing short stories..." - Chuck Palahniuk, author of Fight Club **184 pages $11**

BB-012 "Ocean of Lard" Kevin L Donihe / Carlton Mellick III - A parody of those old Choose Your Own Adventure kid's books about some very odd pirates sailing on a sea made of animal fat. **176 pages $12**

BB-015 "Foop!" Chris Genoa - Strange happenings are going on at Dactyl, Inc, the world's first and only time travel tourism company.
"A surreal pie in the face!" - Christopher Moore **300 pages $14**

BB-020 "Punk Land" Carlton Mellick III - In the punk version of Heaven, the anarchist utopia is threatened by corporate fascism and only Goblin, Mortician's sperm, and a blue-mohawked female assassin named Shark Girl can stop them. **284 pages $15**

BB-021 "Pseudo-City" D. Harlan Wilson - Pseudo-City exposes what waits in the bathroom stall, under the manhole cover and in the corporate boardroom, all in a way that can only be described as mind-bogglingly irreal. **220 pages $16**

BB-023 "Sex and Death In Television Town" Carlton Mellick III - In the old west, a gang of hermaphrodite gunslingers take refuge from a demon plague in Telos: a town where its citizens have televisions instead of heads. **184 pages $12**

BB-027 **"Siren Promised" Jeremy Robert Johnson & Alan M Clark** - Nominated for the Bram Stoker Award. A potent mix of bad drugs, bad dreams, brutal bad guys, and surreal/incredible art by Alan M. Clark. **190 pages $13**

BB-030 **"Grape City" Kevin L. Donihe** - More Donihe-style comedic bizarro about a demon named Charles who is forced to work a minimum wage job on Earth after Hell goes out of business. **108 pages $10**

BB-031**"Sea of the Patchwork Cats" Carlton Mellick III** - A quiet dreamlike tale set in the ashes of the human race. For Mellick enthusiasts who also adore The Twilight Zone. **112 pages $10**

BB-032 **"Extinction Journals" Jeremy Robert Johnson** - An uncanny voyage across a newly nuclear America where one man must confront the problems associated with loneliness, insane dieties, radiation, love, and an ever-evolving cockroach suit with a mind of its own. **104 pages $10**

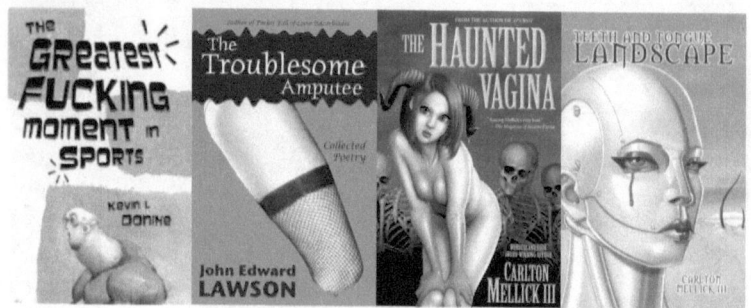

BB-034 **"The Greatest Fucking Moment in Sports" Kevin L. Donihe** - In the tradition of the surreal anti-sitcom Get A Life comes a tale of triumph and agape love from the master of comedic bizarro. **108 pages $10**

BB-035 **"The Troublesome Amputee" John Edward Lawson** - Disturbing verse from a man who truly believes nothing is sacred and intends to prove it. **104 pages $9**

BB-037 **"The Haunted Vagina" Carlton Mellick III** - It's difficult to love a woman whose vagina is a gateway to the world of the dead. **132 pages $10**

BB-042 **"Teeth and Tongue Landscape" Carlton Mellick III** - On a planet made out of meat, a socially-obsessive monophobic man tries to find his place amongst the strange creatures and communities that he comes across. **110 pages $10**

BB-043 **"War Slut" Carlton Mellick III** - Part "1984," part "Waiting for Godot," and part action horror video game adaptation of John Carpenter's "The Thing." **116 pages $10**

BB-045 **"Dr. Identity" D. Harlan Wilson** - Follow the Dystopian Duo on a killing spree of epic proportions through the irreal postcapitalist city of Bliptown where time ticks sideways, artificial Bug-Eyed Monsters punish citizens for consumer-capitalist lethargy, and ultraviolence is as essential as a daily multivitamin. **208 pages $15**

BB-047 **"Sausagey Santa" Carlton Mellick III** - A bizarro Christmas tale featuring Santa as a piratey mutant with a body made of sausages. 124 pages $10

BB-048 **"Misadventures in a Thumbnail Universe" Vincent Sakowski** - Dive deep into the surreal and satirical realms of neo-classical Blender Fiction, filled with television shoes and flesh-filled skies. **120 pages $10**

BB-049 **"Vacation" Jeremy C. Shipp** - Blueblood Bernard Johnson left his boring life behind to go on The Vacation, a year-long corporate sponsored odyssey. But instead of seeing the world, Bernard is captured by terrorists, becomes a key figure in secret drug wars, and, worse, doesn't once miss his secure American Dream. **160 pages $14**

BB-053 **"Ballad of a Slow Poisoner" Andrew Goldfarb** Millford Mutterwurst sat down on a Tuesday to take his afternoon tea, and made the unpleasant discovery that his elbows were becoming flatter. **128 pages $10**

BB-055 **"Help! A Bear is Eating Me" Mykle Hansen** - The bizarro, heartwarming, magical tale of poor planning, hubris and severe blood loss...
150 pages $11

BB-056 **"Piecemeal June" Jordan Krall** - A man falls in love with a living sex doll, but with love comes danger when her creator comes after her with crab-squid assassins. **90 pages $9**

BB-058 **"The Overwhelming Urge" Andersen Prunty** - A collection of bizarro tales by Andersen Prunty. **150 pages $11**

BB-059 **"Adolf in Wonderland" Carlton Mellick III** - A dreamlike adventure that takes a young descendant of Adolf Hitler's design and sends him down the rabbit hole into a world of imperfection and disorder. **180 pages $11**

BB-061 **"Ultra Fuckers" Carlton Mellick III** - Absurdist suburban horror about a couple who enter an upper middle class gated community but can't find their way out. **108 pages $9**

BB-062 **"House of Houses" Kevin L. Donihe** - An odd man wants to marry his house. Unfortunately, all of the houses in the world collapse at the same time in the Great House Holocaust. Now he must travel to House Heaven to find his departed fiancee. **172 pages $11**

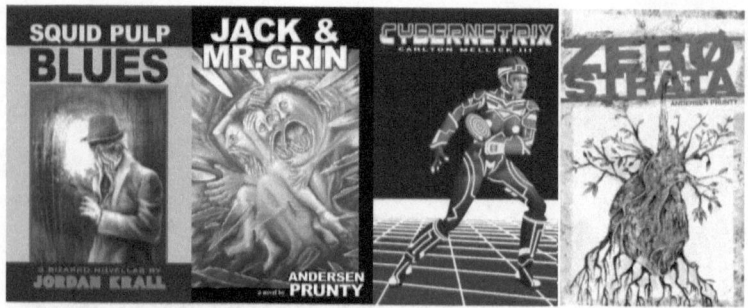

BB-064 **"Squid Pulp Blues" Jordan Krall** - In these three bizarro-noir novellas, the reader is thrown into a world of murderers, drugs made from squid parts, deformed gun-toting veterans, and a mischievous apocalyptic donkey. **204 pages $12**

BB-065 **"Jack and Mr. Grin" Andersen Prunty** - "When Mr. Grin calls you can hear a smile in his voice. Not a warm and friendly smile, but the kind that seizes your spine in fear. You don't need to pay your phone bill to hear it. That smile is in every line of Prunty's prose." - Tom Bradley. **208 pages $12**

BB-066 **"Cybernetrix" Carlton Mellick III** - What would you do if your normal everyday world was slowly mutating into the video game world from Tron? **212 pages $12**

BB-072 **"Zerostrata" Andersen Prunty** - Hansel Nothing lives in a tree house, suffers from memory loss, has a very eccentric family, and falls in love with a woman who runs naked through the woods every night. **144 pages $11**

BB-073 **"The Egg Man" Carlton Mellick III** - It is a world where humans reproduce like insects. Children are the property of corporations, and having an enormous ten-foot brain implanted into your skull is a grotesque sexual fetish. Mellick's industrial urban dystopia is one of his darkest and grittiest to date. **184 pages $11**

BB-074 **"Shark Hunting in Paradise Garden" Cameron Pierce** - A group of strange humanoid religious fanatics travel back in time to the Garden of Eden to discover it is invested with hundreds of giant flying maneating sharks. **150 pages $10**

BB-075 **"Apeshit" Carlton Mellick III** - Friday the 13th meets Visitor Q. Six hipster teens go to a cabin in the woods inhabited by a deformed killer. An incredibly fucked-up parody of B-horror movies with a bizarro slant. **192 pages $12**

BB-076 **"Fuckers of Everything on the Crazy Shitting Planet of the Vomit At smosphere" Mykle Hansen** - Three bizarro satires. Monster Cocks, Journey to the Center of Agnes Cuddlebottom, and Crazy Shitting Planet. **228 pages $12**

BB-077 **"The Kissing Bug" Daniel Scott Buck** - In the tradition of Roald Dahl, Tim Burton, and Edward Gorey, comes this bizarro anti-war children's story about a bohemian conenose kissing bug who falls in love with a human woman. **116 pages $10**

BB-078 **"MachoPoni" Lotus Rose** - It's My Little Pony... *Bizarro* style! A long time ago Poniworld was split in two. On one side of the Jagged Line is the Pastel Kingdom, a magical land of music, parties, and positivity. On the other side of the Jagged Line is Dark Kingdom inhabited by an army of undead ponies. **148 pages $11**

BB-079 **"The Faggiest Vampire" Carlton Mellick III** - A Roald Dahl-esque children's story about two faggy vampires who partake in a mustache competition to find out which one is truly the faggiest. **104 pages $10**

BB-080 **"Sky Tongues" Gina Ranalli** - The autobiography of Sky Tongues, the biracial hermaphrodite actress with tongues for fingers. Follow her strange life story as she rises from freak to fame. **204 pages $12**

BB-081 **"Washer Mouth" Kevin L. Donihe** - A washing machine becomes human and pursues his dream of meeting his favorite soap opera star. **244 pages $11**

BB-082 **"Shatnerquake" Jeff Burk** - All of the characters ever played by William Shatner are suddenly sucked into our world. Their mission: hunt down and destroy the real William Shatner. **100 pages $10**

BB-083 **"The Cannibals of Candyland" Carlton Mellick III** - There exists a race of cannibals that are made of candy. They live in an underground world made out of candy. One man has dedicated his life to killing them all. **170 pages $11**

BB-084 **"Slub Glub in the Weird World of the Weeping Willows"** **Andrew Goldfarb** - The charming tale of a blue glob named Slub Glub who helps the weeping willows whose tears are flooding the earth. There are also hyenas, ghosts, and a voodoo priest **100 pages $10**

BB-085 **"Super Fetus" Adam Pepper** - Try to abort this fetus and he'll kick your ass! **104 pages $10**

BB-086 **"Fistful of Feet" Jordan Krall** - A bizarro tribute to spaghetti westerns, featuring Cthulhu-worshipping Indians, a woman with four feet, a crazed gunman who is obsessed with sucking on candy, Syphilis-ridden mutants, sexually transmitted tattoos, and a house devoted to the freakiest fetishes. **228 pages $12**

BB-087 **"Ass Goblins of Auschwitz" Cameron Pierce** - It's Monty Python meets Nazi exploitation in a surreal nightmare as can only be imagined by Bizarro author Cameron Pierce. **104 pages $10**

BB-088 **"Silent Weapons for Quiet Wars" Cody Goodfellow** - "This is high-end psychological surrealist horror meets bottom-feeding low-life crime in a techno-thrilling science fiction world full of Lovecraft and magic..." -John Skipp **212 pages $12**

BB-089 "Warrior Wolf Women of the Wasteland" Carlton Mellick III
Road Warrior Werewolves versus McDonaldland Mutants...post-apocalyptic fiction has never been quite like this. **316 pages $13**

BB-090 "Cursed" Jeremy C Shipp - The story of a group of characters who believe they are cursed and attempt to figure out who cursed them and why. A tale of stylish absurdism and suspenseful horror. **218 pages $15**

BB-091 "Super Giant Monster Time" Jeff Burk - A tribute to choose your own adventures and Godzilla movies. Will you escape the giant monsters that are rampaging the fuck out of your city and shit? Or will you join the mob of alien-controlled punk rockers causing chaos in the streets? What happens next depends on you. **188 pages $12**

BB-092 "Perfect Union" Cody Goodfellow - "Cronenberg's THE FLY on a grand scale: human/insect gene-spliced body horror, where the human hive politics are as shocking as the gore." -John Skipp. **272 pages $13**

BB-093 "Sunset with a Beard" Carlton Mellick III - 14 stories of surreal science fiction. **200 pages $12**

BB-094 "My Fake War" Andersen Prunty - The absurd tale of an unlikely soldier forced to fight a war that, quite possibly, does not exist. It's Rambo meets Waiting for Godot in this subversive satire of American values and the scope of the human imagination. **128 pages $11**

BB-095 "Lost in Cat Brain Land" Cameron Pierce - Sad stories from a surreal world. A fascist mustache, the ghost of Franz Kafka, a desert inside a dead cat. Primordial entities mourn the death of their child. The desperate serve tea to mysterious creatures. A hopeless romantic falls in love with a pterodactyl. And much more. **152 pages $11**

BB-096 "The Kobold Wizard's Dildo of Enlightenment +2" Carlton Mellick III - A Dungeons and Dragons parody about a group of people who learn they are only made up characters in an AD&D campaign and must find a way to resist their nerdy teenaged players and retarded dungeon master in order to survive. 232 **pages $12**

BB-097 **"My Heart Said No, but the Camera Crew Said Yes!" Bradley Sands** - A collection of short stories that are crammed with the delightfully odd and the scurrilously silly. **140 pages $13**

BB-098 **"A Hundred Horrible Sorrows of Ogner Stump" Andrew Goldfarb** - Goldfarb's acclaimed comic series. A magical and weird journey into the horrors of everyday life. **164 pages $11**

BB-099 **"Pickled Apocalypse of Pancake Island" Cameron Pierce** A demented fairy tale about a pickle, a pancake, and the apocalypse. **102 pages $8**

BB-100 **"Slag Attack" Andersen Prunty** - Slag Attack features four visceral, noir stories about the living, crawling apocalypse.A slag is what survivors are calling the slug-like maggots raining from the sky, burrowing inside people, and hollowing out their flesh and their sanity. **148 pages $11**

BB-101 **"Slaughterhouse High" Robert Devereaux** - A place where schools are built with secret passageways, rebellious teens get zippers installed in their mouths and genitals, and once a year, on that special night, one couple is slaughtered and the bits of their bodies are kept as souvenirs. **304 pages $13**

BB-102 **"The Emerald Burrito of Oz" John Skipp & Marc Levinthal** OZ IS REAL! Magic is real! The gate is really in Kansas! And America is finally allowing Earth tourists to visit this weird-ass, mysterious land. But when Gene of Los Angeles heads off for summer vacation in the Emerald City, little does he know that a war is brewing...a war that could destroy both worlds. **280 pages $13**

BB-103 **"The Vegan Revolution... with Zombies" David Agranoff** When there's no more meat in hell, the vegans will walk the earth. **160 pages $11**

BB-104 **"The Flappy Parts" Kevin L Donihe** - Poems about bunnies, LSD, and police abuse. You know, things that matter. 132 **pages $11**

BB-105 **"Sorry I Ruined Your Orgy" Bradley Sands** - Bizarro humorist Bradley Sands returns with one of the strangest, most hilarious collections of the year. **130 pages $11**

BB-106 **"Mr. Magic Realism" Bruce Taylor** - Like Golden Age science fiction comics written by Freud, *Mr. Magic Realism* is a strange, insightful adventure that spans the furthest reaches of the galaxy, exploring the hidden caverns in the hearts and minds of men, women, aliens, and biomechanical cats. **152 pages $11**

BB-107 **"Zombies and Shit" Carlton Mellick III** - "Battle Royale" meets "Return of the Living Dead." Mellick's bizarro tribute to the zombie genre. **308 pages $13**

BB-108 **"The Cannibal's Guide to Ethical Living" Mykle Hansen** - Over a five star French meal of fine wine, organic vegetables and human flesh, a lunatic delivers a witty, chilling, disturbingly sane argument in favor of eating the rich.. **184 pages $11**

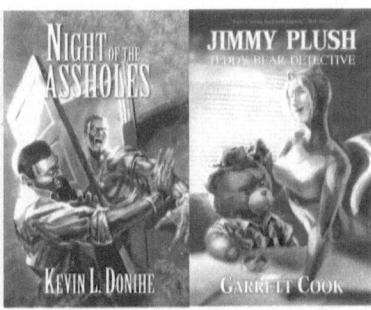

BB-109 **"Starfish Girl" Athena Villaverde** - In a post-apocalyptic underwater dome society, a girl with a starfish growing from her head and an assassin with sea anenome hair are on the run from a gang of mutant fish men. **160 pages $11**

BB-110 **"Lick Your Neighbor" Chris Genoa** - Mutant ninjas, a talking whale, kung fu masters, maniacal pilgrims, and an alcoholic clown populate Chris Genoa's surreal, darkly comical and unnerving reimagining of the first Thanksgiving. **303 pages $13**

BB-111 **"Night of the Assholes" Kevin L. Donihe** - A plague of assholes is infecting the countryside. Normal everyday people are transforming into jerks, snobs, dicks, and douchebags. And they all have only one purpose: to make your life a living hell.. **192 pages $11**

BB-112 **"Jimmy Plush, Teddy Bear Detective" Garrett Cook** - Hardboiled cases of a private detective trapped within a teddy bear body. **180 pages $11**